AT BLACK PONY INN

Alisa Thrau

MYSTERY
AT BLACK PONY INN

Christine
Pullein-Thompson

RAVETTE BOOKS

This edition published by Ravette Books Limited 1989

Phototypeset by Input Typesetting Ltd, London
Printed and bound in Great Britain
for Ravette Books Limited,
3 Glenside Estate, Star Road,
Partridge Green, Horsham,
West Sussex RH13 8RA
by Cox & Wyman Ltd,
Reading

ISBN 1 85304 227 7

One
We buy a horse

It was May. We were sitting on upturned buckets in the stable yard talking about the future. My brother Ben was chewing a piece of straw. Lisa was cuddling Twinkle, our black and white cat. James, who is the eldest, had a school book in one hand, but he wasn't reading it. In a month's time he would be taking his GCSEs, but it wasn't a day for work, it was a day for plans, for sitting around in the sunshine, dreaming impossible dreams.

We had been running the Inn for several months now. We had suffered calamity and found Paul's pony dead and Mary with a broken leg; but Mary was getting better and Paul wanted a new pony, and we had a new guest called Colonel Hunter, who was impossibly old and whom Lisa was always trying to marry off to Mrs Mills, who was a paying guest in her eighties. The ponies watched us over the rail fence. They had shiny summer coats now and their sides were round and full.

"I'm not having this Commander Cooley on Solitaire, whatever anyone says," Ben said. Commander Cooley was to be our next paying guest. He was said to be rich and handsome.

"He's got to ride something. He's coming to ride. It's on doctor's orders, he's had a nervous breakdown,' retorted James, who is the eldest of us and doesn't ride.

"We'll have to buy a horse," I said. "Something large and patient, which will carry anyone – a horse we can trust."

"Dad will only let us have three hundred pounds. We can't buy anything with that," answered Ben. "That's less than meat price."

"Not if it's thin. We'll go to the market – okay?" I asked.

"It's a devil of a risk," replied Ben.

"We'll risk it then." I hated the market. My own horse, Lorraine, had come from there. But we had known something about her. This time we would be buying in the dark. It would be an appalling gamble.

"It must have a vet's certificate and be warranted," said Ben. "We don't want another Apollo.' Apollo had been Paul's pony. He had had a tumour on the brain, which had killed him.

"If we don't get something soon, Commander Cooley will be riding Solitaire *and* Lorraine; and all the horses in *Horse and Hound* are five hundred pounds and then we have to get to see them," I said. "The market is our only hope."

"Okay, Mummy and I will stock up at the CaterMart while you're there," James said. "Remember to ask Dad for the money. They

6

like cash at the market." He walked away with the school book still in his hand, looking taller than ever.

Lisa was talking to her piebald pony, Jigsaw, now. Limpet, the little black which had taught us all to ride, was nibbling her hair. Grey Lorraine was gazing into the distance while Ben's Welsh cob, Solitaire, stood eyeing the buckets hopefully. It was Sunday and the church bells had started to ring beyond the common.

"Mummy says Commander Cooley is tall and slim and incredibly handsome. I expect Mary will fall in love with him," said Ben.

"But he's forty," I objected. "And that's old enough to be her father."

Colonel Hunter was coming towards us now. "He's going to talk about India," said Ben.

But he only called, "None of you going to church?" in a disapproving voice and walked away across the common towards the sound of bells.

Presently Mary joined us, walking with a stick. Her leg was still in plaster after her accident with Apollo, and she looked pale and bad-tempered.

"School again tomorrow," she said. "And how I hate the boys on the bus. Can't your mother take us? Do we always have to go by bus?"

"Yes," I said.

"You needn't talk to the boys. They don't

7

like you either. The dislike is mutual," said Ben.

"Thank you very much," replied Mary.

I didn't want to go inside to help get lunch. I wanted to sit there for ever dreaming about the future, making plans with the sun warm on my back.

"There's a Commander coming in two weeks' time. He's very handsome," Lisa told Mary. "Perhaps he'll take you to school."

"He's got a Mercedes," said Ben.

"And loads of money, because he wants to ride every day and he's paying ten pounds a week extra for the best bedroom," I added.

"Which is Mummy's and Dad's. How do you like that? He's turning them out. I hate him," cried Lisa, her eyes suddenly full of tears. "Why should they give up their bedroom?"

"They don't have to. What a baby you are," retorted Mary, going back towards the house. "They just want the money. That's why they're doing it."

"I wish there were children coming," said Lisa. "I'm sick of the old Colonel. All he talks about is India."

"You can't expect children in term time. Anyway Paul will be here for his half-term in a couple of weeks. He'll play with you."

Lisa was nine, small, thin and determined. I was twelve, with brown hair and blue eyes. Ben was just fourteen and James was sixteen. We had turned our house into a guest house when no one would buy it and Dad's firm had gone bust.

But at the moment we hadn't many guests – just ancient Mrs Mills, the Colonel, Mary, and Paul at half-term. It wasn't enough to make a profit, so the Commander was to be a welcome addition.

We found Mummy inside making a pudding. "We've decided to go to the market next Saturday to buy a horse. There's nothing in *Horse and Hound* which will do. And Mrs Sims has only high-class horses at four hundred for an unschooled four-year-old," Ben said. Mrs Sims was our local dealer.

"Have you tried all the riding schools?" Mummy asked.

Ben nodded. "So many horses went for meat last autumn that there's now a shortage," he said.

"Be careful then,' replied Mummy, who isn't horsey. "Don't buy a dangerous animal."

Dad came in then so we told him our plan. "So you want three hundred pounds," he said. "Can't the Commander ride Lorraine or Solitaire?"

"Impossible,' replied Ben. "You know he said that he hadn't ridden for years and they're as gassy as old champagne at the moment. And anyway he weighs twelve stone and they're only fourteen two."

"Three hundred pounds is cheap, rock bottom for these days," I said. "Lots of people are spending thousands."

"If he rides every day and pays by the hour,

we'll soon have the money back," argued Ben.

"You know things never work out like that," replied Dad wearily. "But all right, you can have the money; but only because I've just sold my big car and bought a little one. It won't be there again."

We screamed, "Thank you!"

And so it was settled. We just had to live through another five and a half days until Saturday.

Saturday dawned warm and fine; and even Ben was up early lunging Solitaire in the paddock before breakfast, saying, "We must be there early to see the horses arriving. We must hear the gossip about them."

Lisa was rushing round the kitchen chivvying everyone. James was making a list for the CaterMart. Mrs Mills was perched at the corner of the kitchen table eating lots of bread and marmalade and drinking an enormous cup of coffee. The Colonel had *The Times* and breakfast on a tray in the diningroom. He had brought his own linen, tablenapkin and a ring for it made out of elephant tusk. He had the same breakfast every morning – shredded wheat, a soft-boiled egg, toast in a toast-rack, butter and a very expensive marmalade, plus coffee in a jug with hot milk and lump sugar.

Ben and I ate vast bowls of cereal, then we found Dad and he gave us three hundred pounds in fivers in an envelope. "And don't lose it," he said. And suddenly I thought again of the risk we were taking and now there was a funny feeling in my stomach.

Ben said, "We may not buy anything, Dad. Don't worry. We're not complete idiots."

But we both knew without looking at each other that because we had the money we would buy something, come what may, simply because the chance might never come again.

"I spent last night reading about choosing a pony. I read five different books on the subject," said Ben.

"Buy a good one then," said Dad. "Or I'll wring your necks." James had brought the Land Rover round to the front door.

"I'll take Mary up her breakfast in bed," said Mrs Mills. "Don't worry. And I'll see to the Colonel's tray and do the spuds. Have a good time."

Mummy loaded boxes into the car, thinking that the CaterMart might have run out.

I said, "Who's got the money?" And Ben said "Me" and tapped his back trouser pocket.

Lisa had put on riding clothes and carried a crash cap. "I may be offered a ride. You can try them sometimes," she said, looking defensive.

"Not big horses, not when you're only nine," snapped Ben.

Mummy started the Land Rover. "Remember that you don't *have* to buy a horse," she said. "There's still a week before he comes."

"But there's only Saturdays; we're at school all the rest of the week," I argued.

"There's the evenings, and Sunday's," replied Mummy. "You don't have to rush. Remember, *more haste, less speed.*"

We had considered hitching on the trailer, but it seemed to be tempting fate too far and anyway Mummy had to go home to get the Colonel's lunch.

It was nine miles to Radcott, where the sale was held monthly in the cattle market. We had sent for the catalogue and had marked possible buys; there was a grey mare of fifteen two which I fancied and a dun gelding of sixteen hands which Ben had chosen. They were both aged. Lisa had marked lots of ponies which we had no idea of bidding for.

There were mares with foals at foot, and harness horses, and a lot of first-class hunters being sold because the hunting season was over.

"Get something steady anyway," said Mummy when we reached the suburbs of Radcott. "Because then Mike can ride it. He's large and quite hefty and we must teach him sometime. After all, he's coming because he's mad on horses, and he will still be with us long after Commander Cooley's gone, God willing."

"Mike!" I cried.

"Not that awful delinquent boy you were talking about, the one the social worker wanted us to have because he was mad on

12

horses and living in a bed and breakfast place. You can't mean it? Not him?" cried Ben.

I remembered now. Dad had said he needed a home. Mummy had said you had to do something for Society sometimes, and this was to be our "good deed".

"But he was a thief!" cried Ben.

"Only because his parents were awful," replied Mummy.

"We're just a home for lame ducks," cried Ben angrily. "We're not a guest house at all. Just think, there's Mary who neurotic and has a broken leg, there's old Mrs Mills who's eighty, and the Colonel who's incredibly ancient and crazy about India, and then there's Commander Cooley coming who has had a nervous breakdown; and now, to crown it all, this terrible boy . . .'

"Why can't we have children?" shrieked Lisa. "Nice children. Children of my age. Like the others we had, like Phillipa and her sister. They were super."

"If you keep shouting I shall crash the Land Rover," replied Mummy calmly. "Children don't come in term time. There will be plenty in the holidays."

"I bet Mike is paying a pittance," cried Ben. "About thirty pounds a week."

"The social services are paying for him, and he's going to help. All you kids are going to eat together in the kitchen, while the Commander and Colonel Hunter and Mrs Mills

13

eat in the dining-room with Dad and me," announced Mummy.

"Crikey!" shouted Ben.

We were near the market now and there were horses and trailers everywhere, mixed up with shoppers clutching bags.

"When's this boy coming?' shrieked Ben. "And where's he sleeping? I suppose you're giving him my room."

"He's going in my sewing room," Mummy said. "He doesn't need a big room. He has hardly any belongings."

There were horses being trotted up and down. Ponies plaited, ponies without shoes. Mummy dropped us in the car park.

"Ring up when you want to come home and say whether you want the trailer or not. Good luck," she said before driving away.

"Crikey, I'm scared. Supposing we make a mistake?" cried Ben, scratching his head.

"Look at all those little ponies," shrieked Lisa.

We went inside. The horses stood in pens. Some looked sad and lost. Others were neighing and bewildered. We walked from one to another. There were ponies from Wales which were two and already quiet to ride. There were young ponies little more than foals, shod, with their ribs sticking out, covered with lice.

Suddenly, I knew I was going to cry. Lisa had stopped talking. "I wish we could buy ten or twelve of them," said Ben.

14

"I wish we had a farm of acres and acres," cried Lisa.

There were old ponies with wind-galls and sad, patient eyes, wondering why they were there. There were noble hunters anxiously neighing, looking for their friends, like people searching for friends at railway stations. There were foals without their mothers huddled together and mares without their foals passionately searching with their eyes. There were lame horses, and ponies with sweet itch, and horses so thin that they were goose-rumped, their hocks sickle and their necks ewe.

"It's like a slave market," said Ben, rubbing his eyes.

I had forgotten that it was so awful. I wished I had brought dark glasses because I could feel tears now pricking behind my eyes. The fitter, fatter horses were plaited and some of the ponies were fat and round and had their hoofs oiled. They all had a number stuck on their quarters. People wrenched their mouths open, talked and spat, and some of the women were crying.

"Come on," said Ben. "Perk up. It's going to start in a minute."

"I can't choose," I replied. "They all look so sad I want to buy them all."

"It must be the same at Battersea Dogs' Home," replied Ben. "We've simply got to choose."

The dun Ben had marked in the catalogue had a wild eye and straight, contracted feet.

The grey I had chosen was light of bone and very thin. "She won't carry twelve stone," said Ben. "I'm sorry, but she just won't."

Lisa wouldn't come with us, but sat staring at a pen of little ponies straight off the Welsh hills.

Outside in the bright sunshine the bidding had started. There was a big skewbald which had belonged to a riding school which we had marked, and a bay which had been hunted seven seasons and was warranted sound. Then there was a mare with a pot belly and deep poverty marks in her quarters. She had been used for pony trekking and was nine, with cracked hoofs and a hopeless expression on her tired face. She was bay, too, with a streak of white stretching from forehead to nose. She was supposed to be by a horse called The Greek.

Time seemed to be running away. The horses were selling quickly. The skewbald fetched three hundred and fifty pounds, probably for meat. Ben bid for the hunter, which went up to four hundred. Now there was only the bay mare left on our list and we started to feel desperate.

"There's plenty more we haven't looked at properly," said Ben.

"If we had come last month, they would have been cheaper," I answered.

"Dad hadn't the money then," retorted Ben.

The mare was led up. "She'll never carry twelve stone," I said.

"She's fifteen two," replied Ben, "and she's got plenty of bone. Look at her hocks. And she's got good feet if they weren't cracked. And her legs aren't blemished."

We were so busy talking we didn't listen to what the auctioneer was saying. We had talked to the mare for a long time. Now she looked at us with her tired eyes and seemed to recognize us.

"I'm bid a hundred," shouted the auctioneer. "Come on, she's a fine mare, by The Greek, quiet to ride. I'm bid two hundred and ten, two hundred and fifteen – come along . . .'

Ben was bidding now. There was a knot in my stomach. Supposing she died, supposing she had an incurable disease, a tumour like Apollo?

"Two hundred and fifty. I'm bid two hundred and fifty."

"There's no meat on her," said someone. "Just look at her quarters."

"Someone should be prosecuted," replied another.

"It's a crying shame," said a woman.

"Stop," I said to Ben. "Stop. We'll never get her fat in time. She'll die. There's no vet's certificate. She'll be another Apollo." I tried to grab his arm, to pull him away.

But he simply started smiling while the auctioneer yelled, "Two hundred and fifty, your last chance, two hundred and fifty, going, going, gone."

'She's ours," said Ben. "And she only cost

17

two hundred and fifty, so Dad can have fifty back."

"We can buy another one with it, please, Ben, please," cried Lisa, suddenly beside us. "There's the sweetest little grey, she's only two at the moment and she's shod, please, Ben, please."

"We can't, we haven't got the grazing," I replied quickly.

"We can tether her on the rough grass in the garden, or on the common — we've got common rights."

"All right, let's look at her," said Ben, and I knew we were lost.

Two
Two wrecks

Lisa dragged us by our arms to the pen full of small ponies. The grey she wanted was the smallest. She still had her winter coat and there were bare patches where she had rubbed herself because she had lice. Her tiny hoofs were shod and the shoes were worn down to almost nothing, which meant she had been worked. I looked at her teeth. She had two in the centre which were second ones, the others were milk.

"Well, can we?" shrieked Lisa.

"Yes do," said a lady in dark glasses. "I wish I could, but I live in a flat, in a street. I can't keep a pony in my living room."

The auctioneer's men started to lead away the ponies one by one.

"She'll go for veal otherwise," the lady said. "To France, cut up into little steaks."

"Dad won't be pleased," said Ben.

"He never said anything about change," retorted Lisa.

We went outside again. The ponies weren't fetching much, forty pounds was about the limit.

"I'll look after her," said Lisa. "I swear to God I will."

A man dragged the little grey outside. She stood huddled with her tail close to her quarters. For ages no one bid, then Ben raised a hand.

I stood waiting with mixed feelings. I wanted the pony, but I kept thinking that we were buying another pony without permission, that it would be another mouth to feed and shouldn't be ridden for at least two years.

Lisa stood close to Ben, her eyes on his face.

"Thirty-five, going, going, gone," shouted the auctioneer.

"We've still got some change," shrieked Lisa. "Thank you, thank you."

"We are not buying another," said Ben, giving his name, and I was glad suddenly that he was there looking old for his age, old enough to be treated as an adult by the auctioneer.

We went to look at our mare. "We will have to give her a Greek name, if she's by The Greek," Ben said. "And the little pony should have a mountain name or something to do with flowers. Do you agree?"

I nodded. Much seemed to have happened in a very short time, too much.

"Who's going to telephone home?" I asked.

"You," replied Ben.

"No, you're the eldest."

"Lisa, then, she can twist Dad round her little finger," said Ben.

We found a phone-box. Lisa couldn't stop

giggling. "Is that Dad?" she asked. "I've got a surprise for you – we've bought two, yes, two for the price of one. And we've still got some change. Yes, a darling little pony for me."

We could hear Dad saying "Oh no!" and "I never gave you permission." But he wasn't really angry. He never was with Lisa. She was one more person he gave the benefit of a doubt. Lisa put down the receiver at last.

"It's okay, he isn't cross,' she said.

"Let's have a cup of coffee," I suggested. "They won't be here for an hour with the trailer."

"Okay. We can't take away our horses until after the sale ends anyway, and they're still selling tack," Ben replied.

Our horses! I thought. If only they turn out to be all right.

The café was full of large farmers. We bought steaming cups of coffee and hunks of lardy cake. "I'm so happy, so very happy," Lisa said. "Let's call my grey Periwinkle. Darling, darling Periwinkle who will never be eaten by the French now."

"Or the Belgians," I said.

"What about Misty?" suggested Ben.

"Or Moonlight?" I asked.

"No, Periwinkle. The others are so common, and we can call her Winkle for short. Or even Winkie," replied Lisa.

We went back and looked at our purchases. We ran our hands down the mare's legs. She looked thinner than ever.

"She's riddled with worms. Let's go to the shop here and buy some worm powder. There's no time to lose," said Ben.

"She's got a sweet head," I said.

The sale was over now. We bought louse and worm powders and then Ben went to the office to pay for the horses. Lisa stayed with Periwinkle. I tried to make friends with the bay, but she seemed lifeless and totally uninterested in everything.

Then James appeared, calling, "Why did you buy two, you lunatics? What good is a two-year-old?"

"She will be a champion one day and she was terribly cheap," replied Lisa.

The trailer was hitched up ready in the car park with its ramp down. The bay mare loaded quite well after some hesitation, but it took us all pushing and shoving to get Periwinkle in.

But at last the ramp was up and we were driving away through the bright May afternoon.

"I must say you seem to have bought two wrecks," Mummy said.

"They will soon pick up. The summer grass will fatten them, they just need worming," replied Ben, speaking like an expert.

"We don't want any more vet's bills," replied Mummy.

"Just a couple of worm counts after they've been dosed," said Ben, making everything sound easy, "and they will be as right as rain by June."

"The boy's come," said Mummy after a short silence.

"Which boy?" asked Ben.

"Mike. The social worker wanted tomorrow off to go somewhere with her boy friend, so she brought him today," replied Mummy. "And the Commander's cases have come and lots of mysterious boxes, so I hope he isn't going to come early too."

"If he does it will mean more money," replied Ben. "And we need money."

"What's Mike like?" I asked.

"Large and strong. He said he would do the tack for you. His grandfather worked at Newmarket," replied Mummy.

Things seemed to be happening fast. It was as though everything had suddenly been speeded up. I had the feeling that the peace of the last few weeks would soon be broken. I was filled with sudden misgivings. I wished Mike hadn't come, that the Commander was only twelve and a girl, and that we had bought a fat horse instead of our poor thin bay mare. There seemed to be troubles ahead, enough to sink a battleship.

We were nearly home now. There were children playing on the common and sunlight everywhere. Men were working in their cottage gardens, and beyond the common everything was clean and tidy like in a picture – dipping woods, soft green fields full of growing wheat, and smooth, summer-coated cows, clean at last after the long muddy winter.

Mike was waiting for us. He flung open the

yard gate. He was large, with a shock of red hair and freckles, and the first thing I noticed were his hands, which were large too.

"I've done all the harness," he called. "I found some shoe polish in the house. It looks super."

Ben and I looked at each other and said nothing. Lisa said, "It will come off on Jigsaw's white bits and on our jodhpurs. He must be mad. No one uses shoe polish nowadays."

"Don't say anything. He's only trying to help," Mummy said. "We don't want to upset him on his first day here."

Mrs Mills came out of the house in her pinny. "Let's see what you've bought!" she exclaimed.

The Colonel came after her. "We're all agog," he exclaimed. "Can't wait to see 'em."

I couldn't look at Ben. "They are cheap and poor. We bought them because we were sorry for them and couldn't afford anything better," he said.

The ramp was down now. Periwinkle was jumping about, so we backed her out first. "Put her in a box. We don't want the others to get their lice and worms," muttered Ben.

"Well, she won't carry a Commander; she's not even polo-pony size," grumbled the Colonel.

The bay mare came down slowly, so that it was easy to see the poverty marks on her quarters, her ribs standing out like the sides of a toast-rack, her distended stomach, and her poor thin neck which made her head look twice as large as it should have been. Ben backed her down and suddenly I felt like crying again.

"Well, she won't carry the Commander either. She's as weak as a kitten," announced the Colonel, turning away in disgust.

"I think they are both sweet," said Mrs Mills, "especially the little grey."

Mike offered to get them water. I bedded down the boxes and they both started to eat the straw. Ben started making mashes for them laced with worm powder. Lisa filled up two haynets. James and Mummy unhitched the trailer. Then Ben and I started to delouse the bay with louse powder.

Presently Mary appeared and stared at us over the loose-box doors. "Whatever have you bought now?" she asked.

"Why don't you help, instead of standing there!" retorted Ben angrily.

"No fear. I don't want to catch lice," she said.

She was dressed in smart trousers and a shirt which had cost twenty pounds. I remembered that she had promised once to help all the time if we would have her back, but she hadn't kept her word.

Presently Mrs Mills called "Tea!" and we shook our coats and went inside to drink steaming mugs of tea in the kitchen. The hall was full of the Commander's luggage with his name on it and a crest. It was beautiful luggage.

"I expect he'll change for dinner," Mummy said. "I hope we can live up to him."

Dad was out organizing the sale of his factory. He had found himself a job in someone else's, which I found immeasurably sad, though he said it was simply "life". You went up and down, he said, and if you stayed alive and had enough to eat you should be grateful.

Ben telephoned the blacksmith. "One is two and definitely needs her shoes off; the other needs a new set – she's fifteen two with biggish hoofs and very poor."

Mike drank with loud sips, putting both hands round the mug. "I'm still on probation," he said. "I have to report to the officer every Friday after school."

"Why?" asked Lisa. "What did you do?"

"I broke into a 'ouse and assaulted a teacher," he said with pride in his voice. "It was the third 'ouse me and my mates had done."

I could see now that he didn't belong to our world. He was like a stranger from another country. I wished again that he hadn't come. "You're not going to do *this* house, are you?" asked Ben.

"Not likely, mate. You're my friends," Mike said.

Mummy was moving furniture from her bedroom to the attic already. I rushed upstairs to help. "I shall enjoy sleeping up here," she said.

"But you won't have your own bathroom any more,' I answered.

26

'I don't care. It's so lovely to be getting lots of money in these hard times."

"Well, watch it. Remember we've got a thief," said Ben coming in, his arms full of blankets.

"He's not any more. He's reformed," replied Mummy. "It wasn't his fault. If you lived in a bed and breakfast place and no one cared for you, you might go wrong."

"Thank you," replied Ben. "I would get a job, or go to school or read books."

"His father is in prison," Mummy said, as though that was the final answer.

The garden was full of flowers. Roses surrounded the front door. Daffodils bloomed under the apple trees, which were still in blossom.

"We need a safe," said Ben, "with a difficult combination."

"We need time," I replied. "Time for our new mare to get fat, time for Periwinkle to grow, time to prepare for exams and school our horses. There's never enough, is there?"

"Mike will help," Mummy said, dusting the windowsill. "He's a good boy really; he's just unfortunate. You must learn to be more tolerant. You always think the worst of everybody."

"We're all thinking the best of the Commander. By all accounts he's a real gentleman, rich and talented. Just a bit nervous, of course, but that's overwork, in the Navy no doubt. But what is he really like, I wonder?' asked Ben.

His arrival hung over us like a cloud. All the next week letters kept coming for him, important-looking letters which Mrs Mills thought must be for her. Then a parcel came. And some new riding breeches were delivered from a shop in Radcott.

We anxiously scanned the bay mare for an improvement in condition. We deloused her again and turned her out in the bottom paddock where there was plenty of grass and Periwinkle already installed. And we decided to call her Cassandra.

Mike came to school with us each morning. Mary said that he smelt and sat at the other end of the bus; but he soon made friends with some boys from the village who were mad on football, and every evening after school he played with them on the common.

And then on Friday a telegram came saying

DELAYED. COMING NEXT WEEK. COOLEY

We didn't know whether to laugh with relief or regret the loss of a weekend's money.

"I hate waiting," said Mummy.

"We moved out of our room days too soon," grumbled Dad.

"It gives Cassandra a few more days to get fat," replied Ben. "She certainly doesn't look up to twelve stone at the moment."

"Well, he's got to ride something. I can't have six horses eating their heads off and not a penny in return," snapped Dad. We stood looking at each other, all on edge because Commander Cooley wasn't coming when expected.

"It's the letters. I hate having to keep his letters and not having an address to send them to," confessed Mummy.

"And it's eerie having his luggage and not him," James said.

"And we may hate him," added Lisa.

"Or he may hate us," I said.

"It all adds up," said Ben, "but I expect he'll be super. He must be if he's a Naval Commander and quite young. He must be a very special person. Someone who can command.

"And who expects to be waited on," said Lisa.

"We're only in a fuss because we've been waiting so long," I said.

"He'll be okay, I promise," Mummy said. "I've vetted him personally and he's a sweetie."

"Touch wood," I cried. But no one paid any attention.

"You're in love with him," shrieked Lisa.

"Shut up," yelled Dad.

"I hope he doesn't come," I said, holding onto the windowsill which, being old, was made of wood. "He's caused enough trouble already – he's bagged the best bedroom, worried us stiff and made us buy a horse. He must be horrible to need so much. I would never think of turning anyone out of their bedroom, never . . . but he has just because he wants a view and his own bathroom."

"And peace and quiet," added Mummy.

I looked out of the window and thought, we are quarrelling about him already, what will it be like when he is here? And I was filled with awful foreboding. I had the feeling that he was going to break us up, pull us apart.

"If we don't like him, we can kick him out," Dad said, putting an arm round me. "What are you afraid of, Harriet?"

"I don't know. I just feel doomed," I replied. "As if he's going to bring us misery. Don't ask me why. I just feel it deep in my bones."

Three
The Commander comes

A letter came from the American boy, Paul, saying that he would be having half-term in two weeks and would someone fetch him? The bay mare grew fatter. Periwinkle shed her coat. James ranted over his GCSEs, yelling at everyone to be quiet, shutting himself in his bedroom hour after hour revising. Ben and I rode in the evenings, schooling in the paddock, improving our dressage, putting up jumps. But all the time, deep down, we were waiting for Commander Cooley, wondering whether he would shatter our peace, drive Mummy into hysterics with his demands, argue with the Colonel, get on the wrong side of Dad. But then when he came at last he was charming. He was tall and slim and wore a blazer with braid on it, trousers, suede shoes and a collar and tie. He said that everything was ideal, perfect, out of this world.

"I know I shall get well here," he said. "Everything is so tranquil, so far from the 'madding crowd', so altogether marvellous."

Lisa adored him. He told her sea stories, and his room was full of choc-bars and drink.

We found him installed one evening when we returned from school and took him to the stables to see the horses. He agreed that Cassandra was still a bit thin, "But I don't mind waiting a few days longer to ride. I've waited long enough as it it," he said.

"You are a fool, Harriet," said Ben later. "I knew he would be all right, but you always get in such a fuss and all over nothing. I don't know what's the matter with you. You've got an anxiety complex or something."

I wanted to touch wood again but I didn't. I was afraid that Ben would see me and laugh. Afterwards when everything was terrifying and the house was bursting with tension and alarm I wished I had. It might have made a difference – one never knows.

The next day we lunged Cassandra and the day after I rode her round the paddock with Ben riding in front. She was very quiet and wandered rather, but followed Solitaire willingly enough. We were filling her up with sugar beet and oats now, making her feeds a little larger every day.

Mike didn't help much. He came home from school, grabbed a great hunk of bread and butter, then disappeared to play with his local friends.

Mummy was worried. She was afraid he would get in with bad company and rob someone. He wasn't doing very well at school either. Ben said he was "just thick". But really I think he was too old and too mature to be shut up in a classroom every day wearing a blazer. He wanted to be out in the world working, buying himself a motor-bike. He just wasn't interested in maths or Julius Caesar.

And so the days passed. Mummy, Dad, Colonel Hunter and the Commander all ate together in the dining-room. Mrs Mills wouldn't; she ate with the rest of us in the kitchen. "I can't hear what any of them say," she confessed to us, "and they won't shout."

Another week went by and now it was less than a week to half-term. Commander Cooley started to ride Cassandra, only walking her at first and promising to treat her like delicate china.

We prepared Paul's room for him. Mary stopped needing a stick and ran up a huge telephone bill ringing up her boy friend every evening. Periwinkle grew fatter. Then Mary suddenly wished to be treated like an adult.

"I want to eat in the dining-room – I can't bear Mike's manners another minute. He eats like a pig and Mrs Mills shouts all the time," she said.

"But of course you can," replied Mummy, taking the wind out of her sails. "And James can too if he likes."

"No thank you, I prefer the kitchen. I can't stand any more talk about the good old days in India when we still had an empire, thank God," he replied.

Half-term was really here now. Paul's room was ready. Lisa picked flowers and put them on the dressing table.

Commander Cooley started to ride Cassandra farther. Once I went with him on

Lorraine. He rode easily on a loose rein. He didn't use his legs at all, but sang a lot and talked to Cassandra. As for the mare, she was putting on weight all the time and her hoofs looked better trimmed and shod, and dressed every day with Cornucresine to help them grow strong. Periwinkle was growing too. Lisa had got rid of the last of her winter coat with the rubber curry-comb and her lice had gone with it, dead or alive. We could see that she had a fine tapering muzzle now, and a kind eye with a twinkle in it; and her neck was light and elegant.

Then some people rang up and asked us to have their ponies until the holidays. 'We want them fit for the summer holidays," they said.

Ben had answered the phone. "You mean just exercised, not schooled?" he asked. "Okay, that will be twenty pounds a week then if you want them in." He talked for some time. "The ponies are called Sea Cadet and Mermaid," he said, putting down the phone at last. "The owners are coming to see us next weekend. They are called Cummings. Their children go to boarding school."

"Twenty pounds a week per pony is an awful lot," I said.

"Most people charge thirty just for livery," Ben replied. "And Cadet's fourteen two and Mermaid is fourteen hands. And we'll have to get some more hay from somewhere if they are going to be in and you know what that costs."

34

Half-term started on Thursday. Mummy disappeared at an early hour to fetch Paul. James got out a pile of books and started revising.

Mike and Colonel Hunter decided to mow the lawn. Mrs Mills started weeding under the apple trees.

Mary sat about getting in everybody's way. Lisa jumped up and down saying, "I wish Paul would come. Why is it taking so long? I can't wait to see him."

Commander Cooley sat in a deck chair recovering from his nervous breakdown.

Ben and I wandered down to the stable. 'You know the Cummings are coming tomorrow at three," he said. "I do hope they like it here and think we are okay, because forty pounds a week is a lot of money."

"They must be terribly rich," I replied. "I expect they've got a heated swimming pool and a Rolls-Royce."

"I expect so too," Ben said. "Lucky devils."

Paul arrived at eleven-thirty looking just as always – well scrubbed behind the ears, clean, friendly, uncomplicated.

"Say, it's good to be home," he said. "Everything looks kind of different. The horses all look just fine, don't they?"

We showed him Cassandra and Periwinkle. Lisa followed him like a dog, asking him questions about school, about his parents, about anything she could think up; anything to be noticed.

When we introduced him to Commander

Cooley they seemed to become friends at once. Paul called him "Sir", and Commander Cooley said, "I've got some cassettes from your country, you must hear them. They are right up to date, the very latest."

And Paul said, "My, I would like that, Sir." And they fixed up to listen to them together after lunch.

Then Mike came and shook Paul's hand and said, "Pleased to meet you," but without any pleasure in his voice, and Paul seemed to look at him with instant dislike.

And suddenly the scene seemed set, but for what none of us knew. Later we all rode, Paul on Jigsaw because he had grown too big for Limpet, Lisa on Limpet, Commander Cooley on Cassandra, me on Lorraine and Ben on Solitaire. We hacked through the woods, and though Lisa was longing to talk to Paul, he rode beside Commander Cooley discussing the American Navy and what his father did and a host of other things.

Then Commander Cooley took a huge bar of chocolate from his pocket and gave us all pieces and told us that he was getting better every day and how he loved being with us; and then waited for us to say something complimentary back.

Ben looked at me and I said, "It's super having you, too," but I only half meant it, because somewhere inside me I still had reservations about him.

None of us knew, of course, that this was to be our last day of peace for some time. It seemed then that the peace was endless, that the woods would go on being green, the sun shining for ever. We cantered over a hill and the Commander started to sing and suddenly we were all joining in singing "What Shall We Do with the Drunken Sailor" and "The British Grenadier". And he kept apologizing to Paul for not knowing any American songs and Paul said, "That's all right, Sir," his voice full of admiration.

The horses seemed to enjoy the songs and they walked with ears pricked and long swinging strides. And because we were all in good tempers, Ben and I made good resolutions – as we rode – deciding that we would start teaching Mike to ride and help Mummy more, and not quarrel. Then we started to discuss Mary and then suddenly we were back on the common and nearly home.

We untacked the ponies together in the yard and Commanded Cooley rubbed down Cassandra, whistling all the time. Then we turned them all out and stood watching them roll as the sun started to go down above the tree tops.

"Don't forget to come up to my room after dinner, Paul," said Commander Cooley, turning to go indoors at last. "I've got plenty of chocolates and some rare stamps you might like to see, as well as some tapes you haven't heard."

We found Mummy cooking supper and she said, "Wow!, isn't everyone getting on well? Really, Commander Cooley is quite an asset" and the Colonel, who was passing through the kitchen, gave a disapproving snort.

"Don't listen to him," Mummy said. "He's getting very old, poor chap, and he feels out of things, unlike the Commander, who will be back on active service in a few weeks' time. He can't help being jealous, poor old fellow."

"The Commander's sure been everywhere – Malta, the States, South America, Asia, everywhere. He's some guy," said Paul.

Mike stood listening. "I wish we had another telly set," he said. "The Commander and the Colonel always want to watch the BBC. I never see what I want to. At the approved school there were five sets."

"Everybody wash for supper," said Mummy, looking at Mike's hands. "Go on, hurry up. It's chops."

A few minutes later Paul came downstairs shouting, "My money's gone. All of it. My money. I've been robbed."

Mummy was dishing up the chops, decorating them with parsley for the dining room. Mike had disappeared. "Go and look again," she said. "It must be there somewhere."

"I'll help you," offered ever-willing Mrs Mills. "I'm good at finding things."

"It was in my money box; it was locked. There was fifteen pounds."

I felt sick inside suddenly. I looked at Ben. Lisa said, "It wasn't me. I never go into his room. It must be Mike. We all know he was a thief."

38

Dad came in at that moment, looking tired. "Who's the thief?" he asked.

"No one. Paul's just lost his money," replied Mummy, putting the chops back into the oven.

"It's not there," said Paul. "I've looked everywhere. I put it in my money box when I came home and locked it. It's shut, but not locked any more and the money's gone."

Ben went out of the back door. "Let's keep calm," suggested Mummy. "Let's have dinner and then all look. It's probably in a pocket. You probably thought you put it there and didn't. It's easily done."

"Not me. I never do that," replied Paul, and I believed him. He just wasn't that sort of person. Dad went upstairs with big strides.

Mummy started to beat the gong. "Get Ben," she said.

I ran down to the stables with Lisa at my heels. It was a clear evening with a red sky promising a fine tomorrow. Mike was fighting Ben. He held the three-pronged fork in one hand while Ben defended himself with a broom. The horses watched over the fence like spectators at a wrestling match.

"I tell you I didn't," yelled Mike. "And you shouldn't accuse me, you foul b—' He used a word we are definitely not allowed to use.

"How dare you rob our guests," yelled Ben.

"They'll kill each other," screamed Lisa.

"Stop it," I shouted. "There's no proof, Ben. You can't accuse him."

"I didn't take it," shouted Mike, charging

Ben with the fork. They were both sweating and one of Ben's hands was bleeding and Mike's face was scratched.

"Fetch James and Dad," I shouted to Lisa.

Then Paul appeared. "Leave him alone, Ben," he shouted. "I expect it was the hired help. It doesn't have to be him."

And suddenly they stopped fighting. Mike put down his fork and said, "Thanks, Yankee. I don't rob my mates. I'm not that sort. Strangers maybe, but not my mates."

"It was probably the hired woman," repeated Paul, sounding weary.

"What, Mrs Crispin?" I asked. "Not her, surely. She's so nice."

"The gardener then, or Mrs Mills gone dotty. Just forget it, will you?" asked Paul.

Mummy was beating the gong again. "We had better wash," said Ben, looking at Mike. "Please accept my apologies." And he held out his hand.

"That's all right, mate," replied Mike, shaking it. We went indoors slowly. The day seemed ruined now. Somewhere in the house there was a thief. It was a horrible thought. And it couldn't be the gardener because we hadn't got one. It had to be one of us or a guest. My mind went over all the guests. None of them would steal. It was quite impossible; they all had money, plenty of money. And then I thought of Mary, who was always buying new clothes and had only a small allowance from her mother, and I thought, it must be her; there's no one else.

What are we going to do? And Ben looked at me and mouthed "Mary" so that I knew he had reached the same conclusion.

Before we had supper Dad made a speech. He said, "I don't want a lot of uproar about Paul's lost money; most likely it's blown out of the window or something equally stupid. We know we have no thieves here. It's inconceivable that anyone should steal. So I'm giving Paul fifteen pounds, which appears to be the amount he has lost, and if his money turns up, he can pay me back. And I don't want any more discussion, is that clear? The loss is over and done with. Of course if more goes, we will have to call in the police, but I trust it won't. I trust this is the end of the matter."

He had changed into a suit for dinner with Commander Cooley and the Colonel. He looked dark and handsome and I suddenly felt quite proud that he was my father. At the same time I thought, this won't be the end of it, because we are going to go on suspecting each other, whatever he says. I shall suspect Mary and she will suspect Mike, unless she's guilty of course, and Paul will suspect poor little Mrs Crispin who is always so tired and couldn't kill a fly.

"Come on, supper," said Mummy.

Four
"It's the police!"

We rose early the next day, because we wanted the stables looking tidy for the Cummings. Lisa groomed Jigsaw and Limpet, while Ben and I polished the brass knobs in the old-fashioned loose-boxes and swept the cobbles until there wasn't a weed to be seen or a piece of straw among them.

"It's obvious Mary took the money," Ben said.

"We are not supposed to discuss it," I answered, putting the broom away.

"She's always been a liar, and look at the clothes she buys, and the lipsticks and eye-shadow. Her room is chock-a-block with them. And they are not cheap either," retorted Ben.

"She has an allowance," I answered. "She calls it guilt money from her mother for ruining her life."

"It's time she forgave her mother," Ben said. "You can't go on hating someone for ever; it isn't Christian."

I looked round the yard; everything was ship-shape, the doors shut tidily, the buckets in lines, the tack in the tack room.

"Her mother *did* send her pony to the

market when she was away to school," I said. "And that was pretty awful thing to do." We were walking towards the house now, hungry for breakfast.

"But that was years ago," Ben said.

How long was years? I wondered. How long did it take to forgive and forget? Would *I* forgive Mummy if she sold Lorraine without telling me?

The kitchen smelt of coffee. Paul was sitting on a stool humming. "Good news," he cried. "I'm going out with the Commander. We're going for miles and miles, no kidding."

"Going out? How? In his car?" asked Ben.

"In his automobile? Not likely. On the horses, of course. Your father has given us permission. Isn't it great?" cried Paul.

"He hasn't," I said. "Not really?"

"Sure he has. Go and ask him. I'm riding Jigsaw," cried Paul.

Lisa was behind us now. She started to shake her head up and down in disagreement.

"But he might let you fall off," Ben said.

"He's an adult, dope," replied Paul. "And he's no kid, no Sirree, he's sure travelled the world. He can ride too, I'm telling you. He's going to show me a ruined churchyard. Do you know it?"

I nodded. "It stands down a lane, beyond the woods, miles away. It's said to be haunted."

We were eating cornflakes now and the sun was shining, and I thought, Paul's right, the Commander's an adult. What are we worrying about, for goodness sake? What can go wrong? Jigsaw's so sensible, and Paul rides quite well now; he's not really a beginner any more. And Dad's given his permission.

"It isn't fair. I never have Jigsaw now," wailed Lisa.

"You have two ponies, that's why," replied Ben. "Jigsaw's supporting Periwinkle."

"I'll have my own pony come the summer," Paul said. "A real Apache pony. You can ride it, Lisa, I shan't mind."

He was dressed already in breeches and boots and a collar and tie. Commander Cooley was eating a leisurely breakfast in the dining room. It was nine o'clock at the end of May and a day none of us would ever forget.

"We'll get the ponies ready then," Ben said.

"I don't like it," I exclaimed, following him to the stables. 'You know we don't let people go out alone."

"But the Commander's been going out alone for weeks now," answered Ben.

"But Paul's only a child," I argued.

"Dad's given permission."

"But he isn't in charge of the horses," cried Lisa, suddenly beside us. "Jigsaw's being worked to death."

We caught Cassandra, Her coat was shining now and she had a lovely fine mane which needed pulling. She was fat round the middle although there were still poverty marks on her quarters, but her sickle hocks had vanished and her neck was losing its ewe look.

Ben looked tired. "I was worrying about Paul's money all night," he said. "It must be Mary. I want to search her room. It was your room once. Couldn't you search on the pretext of looking for something you lost long, long ago?"

"She might come in."

"I could keep her occupied."

"You know what Dad said," I answered. "No more discussion. We must forget it."

"She'll strike again," Ben said.

"Let's set a trap for her then. Marked notes in the tack room. I've got some five pound notes," I suggested.

"Okay, super," Ben replied.

We oiled Cassandra's hoofs. Her tail was like spun silk. "In a few months' time, she'll be a beauty," Ben said.

"If we can get rid of her stomach," I answered.

"We had better have another worm count. I bet it's still worms," replied Ben.

"Hi," shouted Paul. "Come on, Commander. They're ready."

We held their stirrups while they mounted and pulled up their girths.

I wished I could follow them, but the Cummings were coming and we couldn't do without their forty pounds a week.

"Have a good ride," said Ben.

"Sure will," replied Paul.

"See you later then. Don't wait lunch. We may get something at a pub. Paul would like a Coke, wouldn't you, Paul?" asked Commander Cooley.

Paul nodded, leading the way out of the yard on cheerful Jigsaw who could outwalk any horse, and the yard was full of sunshine and the smell of hay and horse; and Ben said, "Don't worry, they'll be all right."

We tidied up the yard some more; then we went indoors to try to make ourselves look old and responsible for the Cummings.

"The Commander and Paul may be out to lunch," I told Mummy. "They're going to stop at a pub."

"Which way are they going?" she asked, looking worried.

"To the ruined church," I answered.

"They are supposed to leave written instructions about where they are going, in case they fall off," she said. "You know it's on the guests' charters in the hall."

"They won't fall off," replied Ben. "Cassandra is still very slow and Jigsaw's rock safe. Do stop worrying, Mummy."

"Touch wood," I shouted.

We washed our hands and combed our hair, and Mary said, "Boy friend coming?" She was always on about boy friends, though she knew I hadn't any.

I found my three five pound notes, marked each one and put them in envelope, and wrote *Fifteen pounds for the blacksmith* on the front.

"Would you like some eye-shadow?" offered Mary. "Or what about some perfume?"

"No thank you," I said.

It was nearly twelve o'clock now, so Ben and I wandered down to the yard and swept up a few more wisps of straw and tidied up the tack room again; then I put the envelope with the money on the tack-room table.

"That'll catch her," I said. "I've only put weeny dots on each note so you can't see them unless you really look."

"Well done!" said Ben. "Here they come."

A Jensen came into the yard and the Cummings poured out of it. They were large and rich and smelt of scent. The children shrieked: "What a super place!"

Father held out a slim, well-manicured hand. Mother said, "Pleased to meet you, I'm sure."

They prowled round the yard like hungry dogs. The children, a boy and a girl, shrieked over the ponies. "I do so love a grey," the girl screamed.

"I like the cob best. He looks so kind," said the boy.

"We've got two more, but they are out at the moment," Ben explained.

"Which boxes will ours have?" asked the girl, who was called Rosemary.

"The loose-boxes," I replied. "So that they can look straight out."

"Would you like to come in and meet our parents and have some sherry?" asked Ben, trying to sound grown up.

"Super," shrieked the girl. "Daddy loves a stiff whisky."

We took them into the best sitting-room, which is a relic of our days of prosperity, and very smart. Dad was out, so I dragged James from his studies to do the drinks. Mummy was making pastry and her hands were covered with flour. "I'll come later," she said.

Dad's bottle of whisky only had a few dregs left in it, so everybody else had Mummy's sherry. They settled comfortably into the armchairs and sipped their drinks. I felt time ticking away. James is good at conversation and talked non-stop; so did Ben. Then Mummy came in and everyone talked some more and needed more drinks and now the sherry was finished as well as the whisky and I wondered what Dad would say when he returned and found the empty bottles.

Mummy said, "I hope your ponies are sensible. I have a horror of accidents. They don't do anything awful, do they?" And the Cummings laughed heartily and said, "Only the odd buck."

"Mermaid's had me off sometimes, but I'm a rotten rider. You'll be able to stick on all right because you're experts," said Rosemary hopefully.

"That's right," agreed the boy. "They just need work, that's what Miss Smith says."

We could hear the Colonel moving about the dining room now, coughing in an obvious way as the hall clock struck one.

I remembered that he considered *punctuality the essence of good manners*.

"I must fly," said Mummy. "I've got things in the oven."

Time was passing. I started to listen for hoofs, for the Commander and Paul coming back.

"They just need plenty of work and to be mastered," said Mr Cummings. "I'm sure you'll manage." He stood up at last. "They'll come over by box tomorrow," he continued. "We'll send their tack and rugs with them."

"Thank you very much," said Ben, opening the door.

They took a very long time going, stopping to admire every flower. Mrs Mills was watching impatiently from the kitchen window, longing to start lunch. Then someone beat the gong. They shook our hands again. Then one by one they got back into the car and adjusted their safety-belts. I listened, but there were no hoof-beats coming up the road, just the song of birds and the shouting of children.

"Let us know how they go," said Mr Cummings, starting the engine.

"We will," yelled Ben, laughing with relief because they were going.

We waved to them as they drove away, then stepped outside to see whether Paul and the Commander were coming.

"Dad will be furious when he finds they've drunk all the drink," I said.

"I can't help that," retorted Ben.

49

I looked in the tack room and the envelope was still there.

"I bet we can't ride their horses," said Ben. "Do we really look like experts?"

I shook my head. I could feel life getting complicated again, the pressures which were coming.

"We can ride them after school," Ben said. "It's light until ten o'clock."

"What about homework?" I asked.

"We can do that afterwards."

Everybody was eating lunch when we got indoors. Mrs Mills was just starting on her second jam turnover.

"Are they back?" asked Lisa.

I shook my head.

"They were going to eat at a pub. They may not be back for hours," explained Ben.

"The new horses are coming tomorrow. They are called Mermaid and Sea Cadet," I said to no one in particular.

"So we're going to be very busy," added Ben.

Later I helped clear the table and stack the washing machine. It was two o'clock now and there was still no sign of the Commander and Paul. Ben went out on his bike to look for them, but was soon back, shouting, "No luck. They must be making a day of it."

We were pretending that we weren't worried, but deep down I think, we were all feeling the first gnawings of anxiety.

"If only they had written down where they were going," grumbled Mummy. "I think I had better switch the oven off, don't you? There's no point in keeping their lunch hot any longer."

"They said they were eating at a pub," replied Ben. "I told you."

"Our local pubs shut nearly an hour ago," replied James, looking at his watch. "How long does it take to get to the ruined churchyard and back?"

"About two hours," I said.

"But the Commander's grown up and used to commanding men. Whatever are you worrying about?" asked Mary, suddenly appearing.

"Let's go out in the Land Rover and look for them," suggested Ben.

"We'll wait until half-past three," replied Mummy.

"Really, you are peculiar," said Mary. "Fancy worrying about a full-grown man."

"It's Paul," I said.

"It's Jigsaw I'm worried about. I want Jigsaw," shouted Lisa.

We made a pot of tea and drank it. I thought of the money in the saddle room and now it seemed a mean, petty trick to try and catch someone with it.

Mike came in saying, "I smelt the tea. Aren't they back? Crikey, they've gone a long way. When did they leave them?"

"Around ten," I answered.

"Still, the Commander's got some sense 'asn't he? Must have to be a Commander. Stands to reason, don't it."

Usually Mummy corrected his grammar. Now she let it pass. It was ten to four. Ben started to pace the room. James returned downstairs from another bout of his revising. "Aren't they back yet?" he asked.

"No," yelled Ben loud enough to split our eardrums.

James rattled the empty teapot. "He's grown up, anyway. We aren't responsible."

"We are for Paul," replied Mummy, putting on a coat though the sun was shining and the kitchen stifling. "Someone had better stay," she said.

"Not me," shouted Lisa. "I'm always left."

Then the telephone rang. Lisa grabbed it first. "It's the police," she said in a small, frightened voice.

James took the receiver from her. My heart started to beat against my sides like a sledgehammer. Ben sat down holding his head in his hands, muttering, "What now, for God's sake?"

Mummy took her coat off and put on an apron automatically like someone sleepwalking.

"The horses have been found wandering on the B450," James said. "The police want them removed. There's no sign of any riders."

Five
Fifty thousand pounds

None of us moved for a moment, though I think we all turned a shade paler.

"Have they got their tack on?" shouted Ben.

"They didn't say," replied James

"Are they all right?" screamed Lisa.

"No, one of the horses is injured. We had better get the trailer hitched up," replied James.

"But where are Paul and the Commander?" asked Mummy in a bewildered voice. "I don't understand."

"I'll watch the phone," said Colonel Hunter, suddenly appearing. "I'm used to emergencies, dealt with plenty in India. Of course that was donkey's years ago, but I haven't lost the touch. I wouldn't put too much trust in the Commander; he's not quite right somewhere. I've known it all along, but didn't like to mention it. I'm used to judging men. He's never been in the Services. I can vouch for that."

"I'll keep the kettle on and get the Colonel's tea," offered Mrs Mills.

"I'll get some loose-boxes ready for the 'orses," Mike said. "Water and hay, the lot."

Suddenly we were all running in different directions, full of fear and panic. "Which one is injured, James? Did they say?" shouted Lisa.

"No," shouted James, "I've told you once. *No.*"

We hitched up the trailer with shaking hands banging against each other and getting oil on our clothes from the hitch-up part. Then James said, "I'll stay. I don't mind. The Colonel needs support. He's too old to go it alone."

"Get some oats in case they won't load. In a bucket, you fool, not in your pockets," yelled Ben.

I fetched head-collars, cotton wool, bandages. I was feeling sick now.

"Ready?" asked Mummy, starting the engine and looking small and tense in the Land Rover, too small for what lay ahead.

Mike waved us out. Lisa sat in the back, the rest of us in the front. "Which is the B450?" asked Ben suddenly.

"I don't know, but it might be the road to Radcott," Mummy answered.

"There must be a map or AA book somewhere in here," shouted Ben. "Where is it?"

I was thinking about what the Colonel had said. He had said not to put trust in the Commander. What did he mean? He was an old man but he knew the world and the ways of men. I felt cold now. I started to pray for Paul. God let us find him soon, I prayed. God make him all right.

We drove for miles. The roads were full of sightseers. They drove very slowly, admiring cottages and flowers and the sudden glimpse of woods. But they didn't get out to look. We couldn't pass them because there wasn't room with the trailer. Ben ground his teeth. Mummy's hands grew whiter and tenser on the steering-wheel, then Lisa started to moan in the back.

We stopped to ask walkers the way to the B450, but though they were full of suggestions, none of them knew. And suddenly life became a nightmare without end and I wasn't cold any more, but sweating.

Mummy was crying now, which was something I had never seen before. Ben was swearing, using words I had never heard. And the sun was going down in the distance, round and red.

"Surely they could have telephoned?" said Mummy through her tears.

"If only it wasn't Paul. Things always happen to him. Why wasn't it me?" I asked.

"Or me?" screamed Lisa.

"Or me?" said Ben. "I would have phoned hours ago."

"I wouldn't have left the horse," I said.

Lisa was leaning forward. "Look! There are the horses, and there's a police car!" she shrieked. "There they are!"

We threw ourselves out onto a grass verge. A young policeman was holding Cassandra. "I didn't know whether to send for a vet or not," he said. "She's injured; needs stitching, I should say."

Her shoulder had a gash in it, so deep that you could see the bone. She dripped blood onto the grass. Jigsaw was happily grazing but he neighed when he saw Lisa. They both had their tack on, but their reins were broken. Mummy looked at the wound. "We can't apply a tourniquet to that," she said. "We had best get her home and send for Roy."

"What about the riders?" Ben asked, letting down the ramp.

"I don't know. I can't understand it," replied Mummy. "I wish your father was here."

Cassandra didn't want to move. I fetched the oats. She didn't want them either. I was trying not to cry. Lisa led Jigsaw up the ramp and into the trailer, calling him all sorts of pet names.

Ben pushed Cassandra. She moved slowly, at a snail's pace.

"She's shocked, that's what it is," said the policeman, who was young with fair hair.

"Is she going to die like Apollo?" asked Lisa.

"No," I said. "And stop asking silly questions."

Mummy was talking to the policeman, asking what could have happened to the Commander and Paul, giving him a description. Slowly the mare moved, slowly and painfully, while I felt torn apart by misery and impatience, with the Colonel's words

56

banging away in my mind like an electric hammer.

"Someone must have hit her, a hit-and-run driver," the policeman said, pushing too.

He called Mummy "Madam". We put up the ramp, thanked him and he said, "I expect you'll find the Commander and the little boy home before you, Madam, but we'll keep looking until you get in touch."

"Poor Paul," said Lisa. "Poor unlucky Paul."

We started slowly, our hearts heavy, our minds filled with anxiety. "Your father will be home by now," said Mummy.

We had taken off the horses' tack. Cassandra's reins were covered with blood and hair and sweat.

We didn't talk much now, just waited desperately for time to pass, for good news to come from somewhere, somehow.

We stopped at the first telephone box we came to and Ben telephoned our vet, Roy Smart. "He wasn't at home," he told us, returning. "But they are getting him on his car radio. He isn't far away."

"Will she need a lot of stitches?" asked Lisa.

"Yes, and an anti-tet injection," I answered.

"And a penicillin injection and lots of sedative," added Ben, who plans to be a vet one day.

We could see our hills now and the gentle slope of woods beyond.

"We are very unlucky people," said Ben to no one in particular.

Mike had bedded down two loose-boxes. Roy was waiting in the yard.

"Let's see the worst," he greeted us, smiling.

"It's bad this time," replied Ben.

We backed the mare out first. The blood was clotting, but she started bleeding again as soon as she moved. Roy took one look and dived for his case. Mrs Mills peered round the trailer, still in her pinny with a woolly cap on her head. "Is it bad?" she asked.

The Colonel said, "She'll never work again, I can vouch for that."

We got her into the loose-box somehow, then Roy, with a grim look on his face, filled her with sedative and in a few minutes she was standing with her head hanging low, her lids heavy across her eyes. And for a time we forgot that the Commander and Paul had vanished. I held her head, while Ben passed Roy what he needed in the way of needles, forceps, scissors and thread. Mike watched over the door. Lisa fed Jigsaw. Time passed slowly. Mrs Mills brought us steaming mugs of tea. Someone switched on the electric light. At last the job of stitching was done. But there were still two more injections to be given before Roy was able to stand back and look at the mare, and say, "I'll just have a little listen to see everything's all right inside. I'll get my stethoscope."

"He must be listening for internal injuries,' said Ben.

We all fell silent as he listened and I thought how long the day had been, and how it wasn't over yet.

"It's still breathing," he said. "I won't do any internal today, she can't take any more."

"What's breathing?"

"Her foal."

"Foal! I cried.

"Yes, didn't you know?" asked Roy.

So that was the pot belly we had been trying to get rid of, that explained everything. Poor little mare, I thought.

"No. And we've been working her," answered Ben, his voice full of guilt.

"She's all right anyway," said Roy gently. "She'll be foaling quite soon, in a matter of weeks, and it sounds a strong little beggar."

I imagined Cassandra with a foal. She would be very happy. She would have our best field and a long, long rest. Roy's telephone was calling him now. He packed his equipment into his case. "I'll call tomorrow about twelve," he said, starting his engine. "Will there be someone here?"

Ben nodded. I fetched Cassandra a rug. For a moment neither of us could think of anything but Cassandra's foal. We thanked Roy automatically, rugged up Cassandra. "Don't do up the surcingle too tight," said Ben. "It might injure the foal."

"We must get her some extra vitamins. What shall we call it?" I asked.

"Windfall," he answered. "Because it will be one if it arrives, okay?"

We went towards the house calling, "Cassandra's in foal. Cassandra's going to have a foal." Everything seemed strangely quiet. The kitchen was empty.

"Whatever's happened now?" asked Ben in an apprehensive voice. We started to run. "They are in the sitting room," said Ben.

We kicked off our dirty shoes. Twinkle mewed hopefully for her supper. The kettle simmered on the top of the Aga. Everything was the same yet different. Everything seemed to be waiting for something.

I felt terribly afraid as we went towards the sitting room. The door was closed but the hum of voices told us everyone was there.

"They are holding a meeting," Ben said.

"A conference or a council of war," I answered.

We pushed the door open. No one was sitting down. Dad was pacing the room and the Colonel was talking on and on as he always did, advising everyone. Mummy looked at us out of a haggard face. Lisa rushed to me and burst into tears.

Dad shouted. "I wish we had never started this place, and where's the whisky? Just when I need some, it's gone."

"Paul has been kidnapped. The Commander has demanded £50,000 ransom money. Isn't it charming?" said James.

"Have you told the police?" asked Ben.

"We've been on to his parents. They don't

want the police told. They think it's safer without the police involved," James replied.

"What about the money?" asked Ben.

"It's being cabled or something. It's got to be in dollars."

"The Armstrongs are coming over on the first available plane, but there's a strike on and most of their planes are grounded," continued James.

"How long have we got?" asked Ben.

"Forty-eight hours. He's phoning further instructions tomorrow."

"So he wasn't a Commander?" I said.

"You all thought I stole Paul's money, but it must have been 'im all along,' said Mike. "I always 'ated 'im. I warned Paul he was no good."

"I've checked up, he was never in the Navy at all," said the Colonel. "I always could judge a man."

So we had to wait until tomorrow. It seemed like eternity. "Can we look for them?" I asked. "They might be hiding quite near."

"No, don't say a word to anyone about it," said Dad grimly. "And remember, all future guests *must* supply references."

"If we look for them, he's going to shoot Paul," explained Mummy.

Somehow we cooked and ate a meal. Mrs Mills was a tower of strength. Mary was much nicer than usual and Mike insisted on doing all the washing up of saucepans. Suddenly we seemed to have become one large family, except that nobody said a cross word to anyone, and most families bicker all the time.

Later Ben and I went down to the stables to look at Cassandra. We found her lying down and now we could see that the foal was kicking inside her. We knelt down beside her in the straw to say we were sorry for making her work, and she nuzzled us gently and Ben said, "You're going to be here for ever and ever and we're going to feed you nothing but the best, and you'll never go back to a market or any awful trekking centre."

She smelt of antiseptic and I think she liked having us there because after a few minutes she started to eat her bed. We fetched her hay and Ben said, "I feel very old tonight, don't you?"

I nodded. "Years older. I wonder where Paul is and whether he still likes the Commander and is listening to his stories?" I said.

"I hope so. I hope he doesn't know he's kidnapped," Ben replied.

"I'm glad I haven't got a rich father," said Lisa, suddenly beside us, "or I might be kidnapped too. Poor Paul!"

"You ought to be in bed," I said, standing up.

"Do you think we'll get him back alive?" she asked.

"I expect so," I said, "with a bit of luck."

"I keep feeling sick," she said. "I've always wanted to marry Paul. I never told you, because I thought you would laugh."

"I don't think I shall ever laugh again," said Ben, leading the way towards the house.

Six
"He wants to speak to you"

Cassandra was very stiff the next day. Roy came at twelve, at the same moment as the Cumming's ponies arrived. We were all very irritable and counting the minutes passing in an agony of suspense.

"Yes, she is stiff, isn't she?" agreed Roy. "I think I'll give her another injection to soften the pain a bit."

Mike and Ben put the Cummings' ponies into their loose-boxes, while I held Cassandra. Fortunately the Cummings hadn't come in person, but the ponies were awful. First they wouldn't go into their boxes, then they raced round and round them like maniacs, churning up the straw and neighing.

"They're a pair," said Roy, packing his things away into the car. "You had better watch them. Where's the American boy, by the way, gone back?"

"Indoors," said Ben after a moment's embarrassed pause. "He's got a cold."

"A cold, fancy staying in for a cold!" replied Roy.

"Well, I'll be round tomorrow to give her a

long-lasting penicillin injection which should keep her going till the stitches come out."

He drove away and we stood looking at our new lodgers without really seeing them, seeing instead Paul somewhere. Was he gagged and bound? I wondered. Hungry and alone? Was he in London in a dingy room or hidden quite near in a deserted building?

I wished we had told the police, because if he died now, we would blame ourselves for ever.

Lisa was still in bed. She said she couldn't face the world any more and that she wanted to die, because life was so awful. And no one had the energy to argue with her, though Mrs Mills played Happy Families and Sevens with her, and Mummy had taken her up breakfast in bed. I think she couldn't forgive herself for having fallen for Commander Cooley, for having believed his stories and admired him, and then having discovered that he had feet of clay, or, as James said, that he was our "fallen idol".

One way and another we were all at loggerheads. Half of us wanted the police called in regardless, but Dad insisted that Mr Armstrong had wanted otherwise and since Paul was his son, he must have the last word.

Rightly or wrongly Ben and I had no energy left to ride Mermaid and Sea Cadet, so we made ourselves excuses.

"They need a day to settle in," I said.

"And it's obvious the journey has upset them," added Ben.

So the day wore on; all of us subconsciously listening for the telephone to ring. After lunch it was agreed that we should search the Commander's room, and we all went together and pulled open the drawers, which turned out to be empty, and opened the two splendid suitcases which remained. We found these filled with newspaper and stones, which did nothing to heighten our morale.

"So the whole thing was planned from the start," said Ben.

"Yes, he meant to impress us," said James, "and we fell for it hook, line and sinker."

His car had gone too, though none of us had noticed. Mrs Mills remembered him saying it was going to be serviced, but she couldn't remember when. She was looking old today and so was the Colonel.

Mummy took the sheets off the bed, saying, "They might as well be washed. He won't be coming back."

And Ben said, "Only in handcuffs. I bet he's been in prison heaps of times."

"And was without money, which is why he took Paul's," I added.

"The minute Paul's back, we'll set the police on him," Dad said. "Pity we haven't a picture of him."

"But I have," replied Mary. "I took one of him sitting in a deck chair. He wasn't very pleased. I can see why now."

"Is it developed?" asked Dad.

She shook her head. "It's still in the camera," she said. "Shall I get it?"

Dad nodded. "The sooner we have the picture the better," he answered.

Then the telephone rang and we all jumped. James ran downstairs, taking them two at a time. Lisa appeared in the passage in her nightie.

"It's the bank," said James, returning. "They want to speak to you, Dad. It's private."

"What now?" Mummy asked.

"The camera's gone," said Mary, returning. "There isn't a sign of it anywhere."

"There wouldn't be. Our Commander is no fool," replied Ben.

"He might have left the camera," said Mary. "He could have taken out the film."

"But he can sell it. You can always sell good cameras," replied Ben.

"His cheque has bounced," Dad told us in a flat voice, coming back upstairs. "That's a whole month's keep gone at sixty pounds a week."

"Two hundred and forty pounds," said Ben and whistled.

Dad started to swear, calling the Commander all sorts of terrible names, while the rest of us hurriedly disappeared in different directions.

Ben and I went to do the horses, with Mike and Mary close on our heels.

Cassandra was lying down again and the two new ponies had settled down a bit and were eating hay. We mucked them out again and fetched then clean water, and Ben said,

"Someone will have to ring up Paul's school tomorrow, because he's expected back."

"What will we say?" I wondered.

"Perhaps he'll be back by then," replied Ben hopefully.

Dad got out his small battered car, which had replaced the large one he once had, and drove away, and Ben said, "You know where he's going?"

And I replied, "No."

"To fetch the dollars, £50,000 worth," he said. "All in lovely crisp dollars."

"How do you know?"

"I just do."

"Well you shouldn't advertise the fact," said Mary, looking at Mike. "It just might get nicked."

"By you?" asked Mike.

"By no one," said Ben quickly. "Let's go in. It's nearly time for supper and we haven't had any tea."

That's how it had been all day. Our usual pattern of life had vanished and no one seemed to mind. The Colonel didn't even demand breakfast on a tray in the dining room any more, but was quite happy to have it in the kitchen. Our consciousness of time had vanished; we were all waiting for only one thing – another telephone call from Commander Cooley. As for anything else, time could stand still as far as we were concerned. So food didn't taste any more, letters remained unopened, and Lisa remained in bed, her hair untouched by brush or comb, because everything became unimportant compared with the awful danger Paul might be in. I think deep down most of us wondered whether Commander Cooley might be mad. It was certainly possible that he had a Jekyll and Hyde character, that he could be two people – one gentlemanly and charming, the other vicious beyond words, capable of anything. None of us had put this into words, but I think we all felt it.

And then at last, as daylight began to fade and the song of birds became softer and sleepier, the phone rang again. Dad was waiting by it, unshaven, a glass of whisky in one hand. I looked at my hands and saw that they were shaking. Dad said hardly anything. His voice was abrupt. He sounded as though he was speaking to something loathsome and saying as little as possible. Then he asked, "Why Harriet? Why not me?" And I jerked to life. My hands stopped shaking and I found I was shivering instead.

Lisa stood beside me now, still in her nightie, with bare feet. "You're not to go near him," she said. "Please, Harriet, please."

Dad was still listening, his face creased into a frown. Mummy stood in the doorway holding a saucepan.

"Don't give him an inch. Call the police," advised the Colonel. I could hear Mrs Mills making tea in the kitchen.

"He wants to speak to you, Harriet," said Dad, holding out the receiver.

"Why me?"

"Speak," snapped Dad, his nerves at breaking point.

I said, "Hallo, it's me, Harriet." And a voice said, "Listen carefully. I want you to meet me at five in the morning by the old churchyard with the money. You can come by horse and Ben can come as far as the old arch and then hold your horse. Have you got that? And no monkey tricks. I shall have a gun and I'm a crack shot, and you both will die and Paul will too. Are you listening?"

"Yes."

"And if you tell the police, Paul will die anyway. And if I die, he will die, it's all arranged. Do you understand?"

"Yes."

"Count the money first and bring it in a case. I shall open it before I let you go. And if it isn't there I shall kill you too. Do you understand?"

I said I did.

"Five o'clock then in the morning."

"What about Paul?" I whispered.

"He will return to the house within the hour." He put down his receiver.

"She can't go!" cried Mummy.

"*No*, you can't, I won't let you!" cried Lisa, hanging onto my legs.

"Why can't I take the money? I'm not scared," Ben asked. "Why does he want Harriet?"

I was trying to imagine the moment. How would he be dressed? Would Paul be there too?

"I think we should tell the police," Mummy said. "I don't want Harriet to go."

"Nor do I," shrieked Lisa.

"We must make a plan," said James. "I will be there too. I can borrow a moped. I can hide. I can be there in case I'm needed."

"But you mustn't be seen."

"Of course not."

Suddenly the boys were making it into a game. It wasn't real and awful any more. They made it sound as though we were going to win.

"You can stick a nail in his tyre. That will give us more time," Ben said.

And I knew now that I was going; there was no way out. I put an arm round Mummy. "It's going to be all right," I said. "The boys will look after me. Besides, he wouldn't shoot a girl."

"There's less than twelve hours to go," said Mummy in a horror-stricken voice, looking at Dad. "What are we going to do?" And suddenly I knew that none of us were going to sleep a wink all night, that we were going to wake up in the morning drained of all energy. But the boys were still making plans. They had a map on the table now – an old ordnance map which showed everything as it had been thirty years ago.

"We're looking for the hiding place," Ben said.

I leaned over their shoulders and looked too. I saw the churchyard and the lane leading to it and the open hills beyond and the railway line and the road which led to where the station once had been, and then I knew where Paul was. "Look!" I cried. "There!"

"The old signal box!" cried Ben. "Does it still stand?"

The rails and the sleepers had been pulled up and taken away years ago. A young couple now lived in what had been the ticket office. But what about the signal box?

"Nobody goes that way and it stands back from the old track a bit. But is it still there?" cried Ben.

"Yes, it's there," said Mike. "It's all locked up. But it's there all right. I've been past it with my mates. The windows are boarded up."

"The Commander could have ridden that way too," said James. "Now for a plan."

"It's quicker and shorter to gallop along the track, but would he see us from the road?" asked Ben. "And what if we've got it wrong?"

"Exactly," said Dad. "They may hold Paul many miles away. We must get him here safe and sound. That's all that matters."

"And Harriet back safe and sound," added Mummy.

"But can we trust him to return Paul?" I asked.

"If he doesn't, every policeman in the country will be after him. He wants an hour or more to get clear. Probably there's a plane waiting for him somewhere," Dad said.

Time seemed to be passing very quickly

now. As Mummy had said, in less than twelve hours I would be approaching the Commander with the money. I didn't want to think about it.

"Can I dress up as Harriet?" asked Mummy.

"You can't ride. And you're not the same shape," answered Dad.

Mrs Mills made everyone coffee. Dad and the Colonel put brandy in theirs.

The Colonel started talking about the old days, about Poona and the great famines. "I was there when they handed India to the Indians. You know. Greatest mistake ever made," he said.

Mrs Mills scuttled about like a little mouse. We ate a strange meal of bread and cheese, pickles, scrambled eggs and bread and jam. No one seemed to mind. It was eight o'clock now and Ben and James were still making plans. Lisa was reading like a robot, automatically, without taking any of the words in. I went upstairs to the attic and set my clock for 4 a.m. I thought of the crested suitcases filled with stones and newspaper and how smooth and perfect Commander Cooley had appeared, and I thought, I shall never trust anyone again.

The last of the day was fading as I undressed and got into bed. And I thought, supposing I never come back? What will happen to Lorraine? And I saw my own funeral and everyone crying.

Then Ben knocked on the door and came

in. "We're going to have a go," he said, sitting on my bed. "James and I have made a plan. It should be all right. God willing."

"Won't the Armstrongs be cross?" I asked. "You know they wanted the money paid and no fuss."

"They only said not to call the police," replied Ben. "They will be pleased to have their money back. Honestly, Harriet, we have a very, very good plan. It can't go wrong. And it doesn't involve the police. Not to begin with, anyway."

"What is it?" I asked.

"We're not telling you, because if Commander Cooley went mad and kidnapped you too, he might force you to give it away."

"How charming," I said. "Thanks for warning me. I *shall* have nice dreams now."

"If he carried you off we would save you; that's half the point of the plan – it's to safeguard you too."

Suddenly I wanted everything blotted out by sleep. I wanted to wake and know the time had come. I didn't want any more waiting.

"Would you go away?" I said. "I want to sleep, if you don't mind."

"See you at four then. Say your prayers," replied Ben, getting off my bed and wandering away smiling in his paisley dressing gown which was much too short.

Mummy came in next. She sat on my bed and said, "You don't have to go, Harriet. You *can* say no. You don't need to risk your life for Paul."

"I'm going and I shall be all right," I said. "Lorraine is faster than the wind. Anyway, Ben will be near. I'll be all right, I promise."

"You can say *no*. You don't have to go," repeated Mummy.

"I'm going," I cried, sitting up. "I've made up my mind. If I don't I shall despise myself for ever and ever. It will ruin my life. Dad is always saying that you must have *a hand to burn for your country or a friend*. Well, I've got one. I'm burning it tomorrow at five o'clock at the old churchyard. Okay?"

It sounded brave, but inside I was quaking, wishing that Commander Cooley had chosen Ben or James instead of me, longing for tomorrow to be over and done with for ever.

Mummy kissed me and left the room. Moonlight filtered through the curtains. A bird cried lonely in the sky.

I tried to think of lovely things – of horse shows in the summer and the glory of winning, of Cassandra's foal arriving, of all the money we were going to make exercising the Cummings' ponies. But all the time, at the back of my mind, tomorrow waited, lurking like a shadow ready to pounce. There was no way out, no going back, no escaping. My alarm clock ticked the minutes away; soon the night was half gone already, soon the cocks would be heralding another dawn. I slept at last, dreaming of Mike coming out of a bank carrying a case (the case I had to carry) full of money.

"I've blown the safe," he said. "It's all right, no one saw me."

But at that moment the burglar alarm went off; and it went on ringing until suddenly I knew that it wasn't a burglar alarm but my own clock telling me that my hour was nigh.

I drew back the curtains and saw that dawn was breaking; the sky was growing lighter, the moonlight gone. It was another day – a day I would never forget.

Seven
In the ruined church

Mummy met me downstairs. "I've made you some tea," she said.

Dad was in the kitchen. "If you're not back within the hour, we'll send the police," he said.

I don't think either of them had slept all night. Then Ben came down fully dressed, his pockets bulging.

"Ready," he said. "It's time to go. I've got some iron rations. We can eat as we go."

James was already in the yard, tinkering with a moped he had borrowed. The sun was rising. We tacked up quickly. My hands were clumsy and shaky. I cursed myself for a coward as I mounted.

Dad gave me the case of notes. "I shall be watching through these," he said, pointing to binoculars, "and if he touches you, he won't live another day."

Now that I was mounted, I felt quite brave. "Don't worry. I shall be all right," I said. Lorraine was fresh and bouncy. I turned her round and waved goodbye.

Mike leaned from a window to call, "Be careful now," Mrs Mills' bedroom light was on, her face at the window.

I wasn't scared any more. I felt incredibly brave in a mad, light-hearted way, as though I had drunk too much. I rode with one hand holding the case, which was incredibly light for something containing so much in the way of future happiness and Paul's life. And I felt like singing.

The common was covered with morning dew, the brambles magic with cobwebs. There were rabbits everywhere and from the fields came the thick, scraping sound of cows pulling at grass.

"It's a fantastic morning," I said. "Why don't we always get up at dawn?"

"We're too lazy," replied Ben. "I hope everything goes off all right. It's a devil of a responsibility." He looked at his watch and we started to canter because suddenly time was running out again.

"How happy I shall be when it's over, when Paul is with us again," I said. "I shall sleep and sleep."

"Same here," said Ben.

Later I dropped the case and it burst open, and suddenly the dollar bills were scattered over the ground. We were in the woods by this time and daylight had come, but we still had several miles to go.

Ben swore. "Just like Dad," he screamed. "Why didn't he put a strap round the case?"

"It isn't his fault," I cried, leaping off. "I let it slip."

Lorraine whirled round, stepping on the notes. Ben swore again. It would have been funny if it hadn't been so awful. We stuffed the notes back, but they looked grubby and wrinkled now, and there wasn't time to count them.

"We're going to be late," cried Ben, looking at his watch.

"Let him sweat it out," I answered.

"Is it shut properly this time?"

"I hope so."

We started to gallop, missing trees by inches as the sun rose, our ponies racing each other, our blood racing through our veins. We came out of the wood and now we had reached the lane which led to the churchyard and I remembered that the Commander and Paul had ridden this way together on Sunday, which now seemed a hundred years ago. Our ponies were sweating and on edge; they must have sensed our anxiety and knew that something was about to happen.

Ben looked at his watch again.

"We'll be dead on time," he said.

We could see the ruined churchyard now – the ruined spire, the ancient tombstones. My heart was thudding in a strange way now and suddenly I didn't want to go on, didn't want to face Commander Cooley. I wanted to turn round and go back and be safe at home drinking tea in the kitchen. The ponies became nervous too; they imagined things in hedges, and shied at the dawn sun shining on puddles, and smelt the air and snorted.

"They smell danger too," said Ben. "Are you all right? Do you want some chocolate?"

I shook my head. I felt too sick for chocolate.

"I wish I was going and you were staying," said Ben. "Waiting is much worse than going. I swear it is."

We had reached the broken, arched gateway, where once people had passed on their way to worship. There wasn't much left of it now. I dismounted and handed Ben my reins. My legs felt weak.

"Good luck," he said.

I patted Lorraine and said, "Wait for me, I shall be back," hoping that the words would give me courage.

The old churchyard is a ghostly place at the best of times. Today everything seemed ten times worse. I stepped over the old broken tombstones clutching the case, and as I walked I prayed, "God make everything all right."

Behind me the ponies snorted and in front of me I could see the hills calm and beautiful in the morning light, white where the chalk showed through, untouched by time. I thought of the Romans who had marched across them centuries ago and how little really changes. If only they could speak, I thought, and then I had reached what was left of the church, and there were steps leading down into the ruin proper and ivy wrapping itself round everything which stood or grew. And I knew that I had to go down the steps.

For a moment, I couldn't see anything. My

eyes wouldn't focus properly and my brain wouldn't concentrate. Then I saw the Commander perched high up in the ruined spire, surveying the countryside through binoculars. He looked very tall, like someone on the look-out of a ship, I thought; and suddenly I was frightened for James, lurking somewhere in his workman's clothes on the moped.

The Commander had changed – gone was the elegance. He was still in his riding breeches, but they looked as though he had slept in them. His hair was uncombed and his face unshaven. He wore an anorak over a shirt without a tie.

I shouted, "Good morning, Commander." And he turned quickly, as quickly as an animal suddenly scared.

"Have you brought it?" he said, climbing down.

His voice was different too. Before it had seemed so cultured, as though its owner had taken elocution lessons, or been to a posh school. Now it was rougher, matching his appearance. I had the feeling that I was meeting the *real* Commander for the first time and it wasn't a nice feeling.

I pointed to the case. My hands were shaking.

"Follow me then," he said.

"But it's here," I answered, holding out the case, longing to get back to Ben and safety. "Take it, please," I pleaded, and my voice came out shaky and I realized how frightened

I was, more frightened than I had ever been before.

The binoculars were round his neck now and I saw that he had a gun, and his eyes looked strange and scared as though his whole life was at stake.

I followed him, remembering how we had welcomed him, waited on his every whim. What fools we had been!

I could see his car now, parked at the side of the road. He stopped where the ground sloped and there were trees. His hands were shaking too.

"Open it," he said.

I thought, he won't be pleased about the dirty notes, and my hands felt numb suddenly and my heart started to race.

"Hurry!" he shouted.

He'll suspect us of taking some, I thought, and wondered whether James was watching now, Ben, Dad, anyone, waiting to help if he went mad, to shout and carry me away to safety, and to home; which now seemed more precious than ever before.

The case was open at last. I held it out to him and heard a dog barking in the distance for the first time.

He looked through the notes quickly, scuffling them with his hands, and I saw that his nails were dirty but that his hands had stopped shaking, as though he knew now that the worst was over.

"Get back to your brother fast," he shouted, slamming the case shut. "And no monkey tricks, I know how to use this gun. I was a champion shot once and I'm not afraid of killing."

Every fibre in my body said "Run". But I stood my ground. "What about Paul?" I asked. "If he isn't released pretty soon, the whole of the world's police force will be after you."

"He will be!" He started to run towards his car while I rushed back through the churchyard, stumbling over the broken tombstones, through the arch, back to Ben waiting with the ponies.

"My God! you were a time," he cried. "Get on, will you?" There was sweat on his face mixed with dirt.

"He made me walk away from the churchyard. He's got a gun," I cried, struggling to mount. But the efforts I had made already seemed to have sapped my strength. My legs were not working properly and there was a hollow feeling in my stomach now. "Let's go home and wait for Paul. He's got a gun. Please," I pleaded.

"It's a mile shorter along the track. Come on!" yelled Ben. "If James has punctured his tyres, we'll be all right."

We raced down the lane, under an old bridge, across some rough ground and onto the track which had once been a railway. The ponies were ready to go. Their hoofs ate up the ground. The wind was in our faces and daylight had really arrived. It was nearly two miles to the signal box, but the ground

82

was smooth and even had an embankment on each side which hid us from the road.

"Still scared?" asked Ben, smiling as he galloped.

"Yes. He's quite different. He's tough, Ben. He's not the same; he's not Commander Cooley any more."

"We're going to find out who he is quite soon and it will be very interesting," said Ben.

"If he doesn't kill us both first," I replied.

We came out of the embankment and now there were placid meadows on each side of us and a smell of thyme. Sheep grazed among bushes. Rabbits scurried into holes at our approach.

"Look!" cried Ben. "Look, over there, you fool. It's his Mercedes." It was twisting along the country road like a snake, smooth and black, ready for the kill.

"I wish we had kept away. He will kill Paul now," I cried.

"He may not have seen us, and he's still got to walk to the signal box from the road which will take him at least ten minutes," shouted Ben, his heels drumming against Solitaire's sides.

"He'll run, and he's fast," I shouted. "He's not smooth, manicured Commander Cooley any more. He's a man running for his life."

Our ponies were almost spent, but we could see the signal box and the sun had burst through and was shining.

"Come on!" shouted Ben, and Lorraine,

who was the fastest, streaked away from Solitaire and suddenly I was alone, racing to save Paul's life. I was travelling very fast but time seemed to pass slowly. And for ages the signal box seemed to grow no nearer. Then suddenly, we were there.

I threw myself off and rushed up the wooden steps. Everything was boarded up, the door padlocked. "Paul!" I shrieked. "Are you there? Paul! Paul!"

And an answer came back. 'Who's that? I'm here and no kidding. Has Dad paid up? Where is he, where's Dad?" He sounded frightened and exhausted.

"He's here, Ben," I yelled, falling down the steps.

"Okay," yelled Ben, drawing rein. "Lorraine has got her breath. Go on to the ticket office. Tell them to send for the police. Hurry."

"What about you?"

"I'll be all right."

I was on again now, galloping, Lorraine's ears giving me courage, her speed giving me hope. Some horses rise to an occasion and will gallop until they have nothing left to give. Lorraine was of that breed. Her ears and neck were dark with sweat, her sides lathered, her breath laboured, but I knew she would go until she dropped. And I couldn't spare her, there was too much at stake – Paul's life, Ben's perhaps even James's as well.

A dog was barking in the ticket office but

the curtains were drawn. I flung myself off and started to beat a tattoo on the door and the dog became frenzied with barking. Then the young owner, who had a beard, opened the door a crack and said, "What is it? Who's there?" He was still in his pyjamas and his feet were bare. The dog peered round his legs, snarling.

"Send for the police," I cried, suddenly breathless. "There's a kidnapped boy in the signal box and a man with a gun."

"Okay," he said, believing me. "Odette, wake up. Go to the phone. I'll go with the girl. Call the police from the phone-box. Hurry!" he yelled.

Odette had hair which hung fair and straight down her back. She was pulling on slacks already, while the man with the beard picked up a double-barrelled gun, boots and a coat. "Okay," she said, "but I'll have to take Matthew."

"Okay, but hurry. Just dial 999." The man was running along the track now ahead of me. "We are not on the telephone," he shouted. "She's got to go to the phone-box."

Lorraine had her second wind by now and felt ready to go for ever.

Then I saw a sight that sickened me – the Mercedes parked less than a hundred yards from the signal box and the Commander running across the ground that separated him from Paul and Ben.

I started to gallop then and the man with the beard called, "Wait for me. I've got a gun." But I couldn't wait. My head felt full of hammers now, hammers which banged, "He's going to kill them, kill them, kill, kill, kill."

But the feel of Lorraine under me gave me courage, because there is something about being on a horse which makes you feel invincible. I can't describe it but it exists, any horseman will tell you this is true. So I felt untouchable as though no bullet could hit me as I galloped on, and the morning was like any other morning, full of the song of birds and the smell of a summer day, except for what was about to happen by the signal box.

Eight
"Have they found James?"

Ben was halfway up the steps. The Commander had him covered with a gun and there was someone else there too – a squat man with a squashed nose, wearing a dark hat, and he had a gun too.

"Shoot them both," said the Commander. "That way they won't talk."

"Not to kill," replied the squat man. "Let's get back to the car. We've got the money. I don't want to be had for murder. Shoot at his feet."

They raised their guns to shoot at Ben, but at the same moment the young man fired. He was too far away to hit them, but they must have imagined he was the police, for they turned and ran. And suddenly we were all there at the signal box, struggling with the door. "But they've still got the money," cried Ben. "Are the police coming?"

"Any minute," said the man with the beard.

"And where is James?" I asked.

"They must have got him," replied Ben.

The door was cracking, splintering under our combined efforts. The young man gave one final crashing blow with the butt of his gun and then we were inside staring at Paul, bound to the seat where a signal man had sat in happier times.

He was very pale. "Have they gone?" he asked. "Have they got the money?"

Ben nodded. "Listen!" he said, "Police sirens."

I went to the steps and looked out. There were police cars parked along the roadside, policeman running towards the signal box, and the girl running with the dog, Matthew, strapped to her back.

Ben had untied Paul by this time. The young man was rubbing his wrists saying, "It's just the circulation. They'll be all right in a minute."

"He was some crook," said Paul through chattering teeth. "Is Dad coming?"

"There's been a strike – all planes grounded – but he'll be here," said Ben. And all the time the police were coming nearer while I stood scanning the horizon, searching for James on his moped, seeing no sign of him anywhere.

"Was James to come here?" I asked.

"Yes," replied Ben, suddenly beside me.

"Where can he be then?"

"I don't know."

Our ponies were cropping the grass below. They looked a sorry sight, soaked in sweat and mud, their flanks run up like greyhounds. Then Ben came to life and leapt down the steps and ran towards the police shouting. "He's got away in a black

Mercedes, number plate MOP 934L. He's got £50,000 on board and perhaps my brother. There's two of them."

Some of the police were running back now, talking into their walkie-talkie sets. And Paul was sitting on the steps saying, "I want my parents. Why haven't they come?"

"The planes are grounded," I said.

"But there isn't any fog."

"There's a strike."

And then suddenly there were more people coming. Mummy and Dad and two larger figures, and the Colonel hurrying behind. And I started to wave and shout, "Paul's all right. He's here."

And Mummy rushed up the steps crying. "Thank God you are safe, Harriet. I've been so frightened," while Ben went on talking to the police.

Then I saw that the other figures were Mr and Mrs Armstrong and I turned to Paul and yelled, "Your parents are here. They've come!"

He looked at me in a dazed way and said, "My parents. Here?"

"Yes," I yelled. "Here!"

And then he stood up and began to shout, "Mom. Dad. I'm here. I'm all right. But he was some crook, no kidding."

And Mrs Armstrong was running now with outstretched arms, while the Colonel stood waving his stick and shouting, "Where's the other one? The dark-haired lad. The one who went out on the moped."

And I shouted, in a voice which was suddenly not my own any more, "I don't know."

Some of the police stayed but most of them went away. There was a policewoman who questioned Paul in a soothing voice and a young constable who wrote down everything Paul said. Other policemen disappeared with Dad while the girl from the ticket office brought us hot coffee in a Thermos. I was feeling very cold by this time and I kept worrying about James. The policewoman asked me a few questions about Commander Cooley and then Mummy said, "Ben has gone in one of the pandas. Can you manage to get both the ponies back, Harriet? Are you sure, absolutely sure?" And I kept nodding, though I wasn't sure at all, because suddenly everything seemed unreal and I was worrying so terribly about James.

"I think he's mad," I said, catching Lorraine.

"Who?"

"Commander Cooley. His eyes are mad, anyway." Mummy held Solitaire while I mounted.

"I must go back with Paul and his parents; they only landed an hour ago," she said. "Please be careful." She looked desperately tired, more tired than she had ever looked before.

"I shall be all right," I said. "I just wish we knew where James was."

"He was supposed to puncture the tyres, apparently," Mummy said.

"And the other man was there and caught him," I cried, turning towards home, not wanting to think further.

"The police will find him" said Mummy without any conviction in her voice.

Dead or alive, I thought, riding along the track, not seeing it, not seeing anything very much any more. I was very tired. I hadn't eaten anything since the night before. But the ponies understood. They looked after me. They went like angels. I think I cried into Lorraine's mane. I can't remember much of the journey. I think Lorraine simply carried me home.

I know it seemed like midday as I passed the old familiar common, high now in grass, sweet with the scent of flowers from cottage gardens.

I thought, we didn't do the right things. We didn't really save Paul because they were going to let him go anyway, and now we've lost James and that's even worse because we haven't £50,000 like the Armstrongs. And my mind was full of mad, muddled thoughts which seemed to glide into each other without making any sense, so that I felt like a ship without a rudder, drifting hopelessly without guidance in a strong sea. The ponies didn't trot – perhaps they thought I was too weak to stay on; they walked with long swinging strides, proud and independent, taking me home.

I thought, perhaps James is home waiting for us, perhaps he's all right after all, as the

91

ponies turned through the gateway and there
was the dear familiar yard all bathed in sunlight and a little knot of people seemingly
waiting for me, their faces smiling. It was
like a dream, but it wasn't – it was real.

There was Roy smiling, and Mrs Mills in
her woolly cap, and Mike with his big hands
all red and soapy. And Lisa laughing and
proud. I seemed to be seeing them all for the
first time, as though I had been away a long
time and come back. I wanted to say,
"Where's James?" But no words would come.

Mike took hold of Solitaire.

"Come and look," shrieked Lisa. "Cassandra's had a foal. It was a bit of a job, but it's
all right, a lovely little colt, isn't it, Roy?"

"It was a real cliff-hanger but they are both
all right," said Roy. "But what's happened to
you?"

His face seemed to be going away; they all
were, growing smaller and smaller. I forced
my legs to dismount. I tried to say "Hurray!"
or "Thank you." Something appropriate. But
now they were far away and there didn't
seem any point in shouting.

I felt my feet touch the ground, then they
crumpled and I thought, you're fainting,
head between your knees, you fool; and
everything went black and I passed out.

Roy was leaving when I came round and I
was sitting in a chair in the kitchen with
Mrs Mills making tea, and Mary was saying,

"Cold towels on her face will bring her round."

Roy was just the same as ever, with his wellington boots turned down at the top and his rugged face smiling, all crooked and agreeable, and so strong that one knew he was capable of facing almost anything and coming through all right.

"What happened? Where are the others?" cried Lisa, her small face close to mine.

"Has anyone seen to the horses?" I asked.

"Mike has. He's a good boy, that one," shouted Mrs Mills. "Here, have this. There's lots of sugar in it." She handed me a cup of tea.

I wanted to say, "I hate sugar," but I knew she wouldn't hear because she wasn't wearing her hearing-aid.

"Look after yourself. Bye for now," said Roy, slamming the back door after him.

"He carried you. I think he kissed you. He must want to marry you," said Lisa, who is full of silly ideas culled from sloppy television programmes.

The tea had brandy in it. It burnt my throat, but gradually I felt strength coming back.

"What about the others?" asked Lisa in a small, frightened voice. "Where are they?"

"With the police. All right, except for James; he's lost."

"What about Paul?"

"He's okay. Shaken but all right," I replied.

"It's James who is lost. I think they've got him."

I knew I was going to cry and I didn't want Mary to see me crying. Mrs Mills handed me a thick wedge of fruit cake. "It's full of iron," she shouted. "Eat it up."

"Why doesn't the old b— put on her hearing-aid?" asked Mary.

"Don't be beastly," shrieked Lisa.

"What's she saying?" asked Mrs Mills, putting her face near mine so that she could hear.

"Nothing," I shouted.

I wished the others would come home. Mary seemed so spiteful, and Lisa was silly and Mrs Mills deaf. I stood up. "I'm all right now. I'm going to see to the horses," I said, sniffing. "I want to look at the foal."

I went outside and thought that James might be dead and no one seemed to care.

Mike was working on Solitaire and Lorraine, drying them with straw, hissing like a groom of long ago.

I told him what had happened, how the Commander had changed, and that Paul was all right but James was lost. I told him the police had taken over now and he kept nodding and saying things like "Well done" and "That's all right then." Things which really didn't mean anything at all.

"They came straight 'ere," he said. "Straight off the plane."

"They?" I asked.

"Paul's parents."

"They were in a proper state, they were."

I stood looking at Cassandra's foal. He was strong and roan, with a white streak on his face just like his mother. Mike had made Cassandra a bran mash and her box was bedded deep with straw. She looked very proud and happy, and peaceful too, as though all her misery was forgotten and only happiness lay ahead.

Mike and I turned Lorraine and Solitaire out and watched them roll. Morning seemed long ago now, like a dream, like something which had never happened. I was missing Ben now. When we went indoors Mrs Mills was laying the table for tea and the kettle was bubbling on the Aga.

"They must be back soon," she shouted.

And presently a young man came and started photographing the house and asking questions. He had long hair and a fantastic Grecian nose and Lisa fell for him at once and told him all about Paul. He took some photographs and gave Lisa a box of chocolates before he vanished, and it was only afterwards we realized he was a reporter and that now everything would be in the papers. And I remembered that the Armstrongs didn't want any fuss, and no publicity, and I felt like screaming.

Then Mike came in and said, "A man's been photographing the stables and asking questions. He gave me this," and held out a five pound note. "Is he a cop?"

95

"A reporter, you fool," said Mary. "You shouldn't have told him anything."

I went upstairs to my room because I was tired of the others, and I lay on my bed and thought, what if James never comes back? And then I think I must have slept, for the next thing I knew Mummy was shaking me, saying, "Are you all right, Harriet?"

She had dark smudges of exhaustion under her eyes and she had put on an apron which smelt of onions.

"Isn't it lovely about the foal?" she asked.

"Have they found James?" I asked, sitting up.

"No. But they're looking," she said.

Nine
"Will it leave a scar?"

I joined everyone downstairs. The Armstrongs had gone to a hotel for baths and a proper meal. Paul had a police guard. Ben was telling everybody what had happened. He looked very tired, but strung up too, so that one knew he wouldn't rest until James was found.

Dad was upstairs with two policemen, going through the Commander's bedroom. The Colonel was sipping whisky in the kitchen and talking about the old days. I missed James. Often I hate him, but now I missed him. If he never comes back I shall go mad, I thought. Life will never be the same again.

Mummy was cooking. "You must keep your strength up," she said.

"What for?" I asked. "We made a right mess of things, didn't we?"

"We don't know yet. We may have done all right," replied Ben.

"Not if James is dead," I said.

"He'll be all right. Bad pennies always turn up again," replied Ben, trying to laugh.

"I don't want that word mentioned again," cried Mummy.

"What word?" asked Ben.

"Dead." Her hands were shaking.

"Sit down. I'll cook," I offered. "I'm all right now and he'll be all right, you'll see."

"It's so awful. I was such a fool. I trusted Commander Cooley; I actually liked him. That's what makes it so much worse," cried Mummy.

"In future, we'll have references from every single guest – long ones," said Ben.

"If James doesn't come back, there won't be a future," replied Mummy.

Looking round I saw how dirty we all were; even the Colonel was looking less stately than usual. Mrs Mills had put on her hearing-aid at last and was asking everyone questions. Mike was sweeping the kitchen floor. I sat thinking that I had misjudged everyone. The Colonel had seemed a boring old man and yet he had great courage and endurance. We had despised Mike and thought him a thief, but he had proved a tower of strength, and honest too. As for Commander Cooley whom we had thought such a gentleman, he had turned out to be a criminal. I thought, I will never try to judge anyone again, nor will I give them the benefit of the doubt as Dad always does. I shall be on my guard.

"There's a car," said Ben, going to the window. "Another panda. Oh God! What now?"

Mummy's hands started to shake again. Then a policeman knocked on the door and asked for Dad. He came rushing downstairs and they went into the sitting-room together, shutting the door after them. I think we all imagined disaster then. I know Lisa started to cry immediately without saying a word.

"It's about James, isn't it?" I asked. "If they had found him they would have brought him here."

"That's right," said Mummy, sinking into a chair.

I smelt the ill-fated onions burning and took them off the stove. No one was talking any more, just waiting.

"You should have gone with them," Ben told Mummy after a time.

Colonel Hunter had fallen asleep, his head on the kitchen table. The clock went on ticking. Mike stopped sweeping. "Everything's going to be all right, Auntie," he said, patting Mummy's shoulder. "I promise."

He always called Mummy "Auntie". She hated it, but never complained because she was so sure he needed love and understanding, so that any small sign of affection must be welcomed, even if it meant being called Auntie. Looking at Mike now, I knew she had been right. He had changed beyond recognition. He was sane and responsible now; someone you could trust. So our one and only good deed has worked out, I thought, but I couldn't rejoice, not until James was with us too, safe and whole.

Colonel Hunter sat up, muttering. "Sorry about that – been asleep. Bad manners, I know, just flaked out."

"How do you know it's going to be all right?" Lisa asked Mike. "Come on, how?"

"Because the Commander isn't that bad. He isn't a killer. He's just a con-man," replied Mike as though he knew. "I've met some criminals and they're all different; some can kill, some can't. Commander Cooley can't — he hasn't the temperament."

I remembered that Mike's father was in prison. He never visited him, nor his mother. Had he rejected them or had they rejected him?

Mary was filing her nails. She was the only one of us who had combed her hair since early morning.

We could hear Dad showing the policeman out now, saying, "Thank you very much. It was good of you to come. Everything is in the clear now then."

And Lisa started to jump up and down, crying. "What does in the clear mean?"

And Ben shouted, "Shut up, I'm listening."

Then we heard the panda car start up, and Dad came into the kitchen and said, "Be quiet everyone. I want to tell you exactly what has happened."

But of course we couldn't be quiet. Lisa screamed, "Is James all right? Yes or no?"

Ben said, "Have they got the money back?"

And Mummy said, "Where's James? Where?"

"In hospital," Dad said, looking weary. "But he's all right. We can fetch him presently. He's been stitched up."

"Where? Where is he stitched up?" cried Mummy.

"On the side of his face and on his left knee, and he's cracked a bone or two," said Dad, smiling. "But he's all right, so stop worrying."

"Will it leave a scar? On his face, I mean?" asked Mummy.

"I don't know. It doesn't matter much anyway," replied Dad. "Boys don't have to be pretty and they'll be honourable scars."

"That's right," said Mike approvingly to no one in particular.

"You are all so self-centred," complained Mary. "What about the Commander? Has anybody found my camera? It wasn't insured and I want it back."

"Who's self-centred now?" whispered Lisa.

"Let's begin at the beginning, shall we?" asked Dad. "Sit down and I will tell you everything the Inspector said. But no interruptions, please."

Mrs Mills turned up her hearing-aid. The Colonel lit his pipe.

"The police know all about Commander Cooley. His real name isn't Cooley at all, but plain Mr Smith," began Dad. "He's been in and out of prison since his twenties. Twice for bigamy—'

"What's bigamy, eh?" interrupted Lisa.

"Getting married when you are *already* married," replied Mummy.

"I thought that was called divorce," said Lisa.

"Shut up," shouted Ben.

"He was in the Navy for a short time as

an ordinary seamen but was discharged for theft," continued Dad. "Since then he has been kept by various women who imagined they were his lawful wives. Two years ago he was jailed for bigamy for the second time and for cashing dud cheques, but since he is always a model prisoner he was soon released and soon collected some money from somewhere and came here. No one knows how he discovered that Paul would be here, but he obviously did before he came because the whole kidnap plan was set very carefully. We don't know where the Mercedes came from either, but it was probably stolen at some time or other."

"Or belonged to the other man, the one with the funny nose," cried Ben. "What about him?"

"He was in prison before the Commander, I mean plain Mr Smith," replied Dad. "And he lives five miles from here and came out six months ago, so he probably told Mr Smith about Paul. All that will come out in court."

"Will we have to give evidence in court?" asked Ben.

"I expect so, but I gather someone has already given an interview to the press," said Dad, looking at Lisa with a slight smile on his lips.

"I didn't mean to. I didn't know he was a reporter," said Lisa, blushing. "He came and asked questions, and was so nice I think I want to marry him!"

"You know Lisa," I cried. "A charming

man has only to smile at her and she tells all."

"What about the money? I keep asking, but you never say," complained Ben.

"It was in the car, intact. The Armstrongs are taking it with them tomorrow when they fly out."

"Fly out?" cried Lisa. "Paul isn't leaving, is he?"

"Yes, they are taking him with them. Now that the news has broken they are afraid someone else will have a go at kidnapping him. And they haven't had much luck, have they? First they're sold a dud pony, then Paul's kidnapped. You can't say old England's treated them very well," said Dad.

"Won't he ever come back? Is he coming to say goodbye?" asked Lisa in a tearful voice.

"Yes, tomorrow. We have to pack his things up," Dad said.

It was like the end of a chapter; our relationship with Paul was over; but I couldn't blame the Armstrongs for taking him away, for he had had enough frights to last a lifetime.

"He didn't want to go. He was crying his eyes out," Dad continued. "But he'll like it when he gets there."

"What, in an apartment?" cried Lisa.

"They're buying a farm," replied Dad.

It was eight o'clock now. Mummy stared at the clock in dismay. "I haven't done anything about dinner. I haven't even taken the meat out of the deep freeze. It's still frozen," she cried, leaping up. "I've done nothing but cook onions. I must be mad."

"I'm quite happy with scrambled eggs," said Mrs Mills.

"I'm not. I'm dying on my feet from hunger," replied Ben.

"All I want is a nice drink," said Dad, "and there isn't any drink."

"I want you to be my guests," said the Colonel rather loudly. "I may be an old man but I'm not a poor one. Will you do me the honour of dining with me tonight?"

"What, all of us?" asked Ben.

"Yes, all of you."

"Me too?" asked Mrs Mills.

"Not me, sir. I've never eaten in a restaurant before," said Mike.

Colonel Hunter held out his hand. "I'm proud to know you, Mike," he said. "If you were in my regiment I would recommend you for promotion. You are the salt of the earth, sir. Of course you are coming."

Mike took his hand, blushing to the roots of his carrot-coloured hair.

Lisa cried, "What shall I wear? My one and only dress is filthy."

"We had better see to the horses first," I said to Ben. "You know our rule, 'horses before humans', and Solitaire and Lorraine were marvellous."

We remembered then that we hadn't looked at the Cummings' ponies all day. "They'll have azoturia, from not being exercised," I cried. "We'll have to take them out now. We can't go out to dinner, that's all. It's still light."

"And I love a good dinner," wailed Ben. "And I've had nothing but a sausage roll and a cup of tea for hours and hours."

"We exercised them," said Lisa. "So stop worrying."

"You?" cried Ben.

"She said they would get some frightful complaint, something beginning with 'a'," said Mike. "So we lunged them. We looked it up in a book and we found the lunging rein and Ben's old hunting whip."

"They were awful. Cadet bucked and bucked, but Mike was marvellous," Lisa related.

"We gave them twenty minutes each and most of it was trotting; then we grazed them along the roadside for a bit; then Cassandra started her labour pains – at least that's what Mrs Mills called them," Mike said.

"We fetched her for advice. We didn't know what to do. Cassie kept lying down and getting up," continued Lisa.

"We looked up foaling in a book. It said a mare mustn't be in labour more than half an hour, so we rang up Roy," Mike said.

"It was a very bad birth, according to Roy," continued Lisa, sounding grown up and knowledgeable. "The foal got stuck and we had to use a rope on it. Mrs Mills was marvellous, she held Cassandra all the time. You would never think she was eighty-something."

Suddenly I saw that Lisa was growing up; that she wasn't just a tiresome little sister any more. She was capable of responsibility too.

Ben was staring at them both. "Cassandra would have died without you. Thank God you were here. And thank you for lunging the Cummings' ponies," he said.

"It was a pleasure," replied Mike. "And you needn't check anybody's water buckets. I was out there at seven and I checked everything."

"Stop gossiping and get ready," called Dad. "Wash your hands. And clean your nails, Ben. We don't want the smell of stable wherever we're going. And put on a dress, Harriet. I'm going to fetch James. I'll be back in half an hour."

Colonel Hunter was on the telephone trying to book a table somewhere. But he had to telephone three places before he could find anybody who would have us all.

Mrs Mills was muttering, "I hope my suit will do," and frantically washing up cups which didn't need washing.

Mary had locked herself in the bathroom so that no one else could wash. Ben started to clean his shoes. I looked through my dresses. They were all too small, but there wasn't time to let them down.

Outside the ponies were grazing. The sun was going down. It seemed the longest day of my life and it wasn't over yet.

Ten
The Colonel's dinner party

Dad telephoned to say he would meet us at the hotel; he said that James was all right but still a bit sleepy, and not to worry. So the rest of us piled into the Land Rover, Colonel Hunter sitting in the front with Mummy, who was driving, and the rest of us in the back – Mary, myself and Lisa on one side, Ben, Mike and Mrs Mills on the other.

Only Mary was smart. My dress was too short and my ankle socks kept disappearing into my sandals, which were too small. My only other respectable clothes were my school uniform – sensible black shoes, dark socks or stockings, a ghastly skirt and blouse, and a blazer with a stupid crest on it. Otherwise my clothes were old trousers or for riding. Mrs Mills had on a suit which smelt of mothballs, and one of her strange woolly caps, and sensible lace-up shoes which had been handmade twenty years ago.

Ben was wearing his riding coat, school trousers and jodhpur boots, and a very clean white shirt. His hands were clean, but he hadn't washed his face, which I was sure Mummy would notice any minute, and his neck looked decidedly grubby against his white shirt. Mike had put on his school clothes – trousers, a shirt, blazer, school tie and black shoes – but since the social services had provided them secondhand, none of them really fitted.

Mary wore a long skirt, an embroidered blouse, earrings, fashionable shoes, and smelt delicious. She made me feel very young and gauche.

The Colonel kept telling Mummy which way to go, though she knew already. Mrs Mills lectured us on the versatility of Land Rovers. Mary tried to chat up Ben, but quite soon he fell asleep with his mouth open.

I wondered where the Commander was now and tried to imagine him handcuffed in a cell. I wondered why he had made such a mess of his life when he was both good-looking and clever. Then Mary started to grumble. "When are we going to arrive? This thing shakes you to pieces," she said. "And I bet the old Colonel's a frightful bore when we get there."

"He's jolly nice to have us. Dinner will be at least a hundred pounds," I said.

"Well it hasn't been much of a day, has it?" grumbled Mary. "No proper lunch or tea, and just Mrs Mills doing all the work. Call yourself a guest house."

"You can always leave," said Ben, waking up. "We don't need you. We are perfectly happy with the Colonel and Mrs Mills and Mike until the holidays start."

We could see the hotel now, large and splendid, with a great sweep of drive and high Georgian windows. Lisa started to jump about. "Do you think he'll let me drink? I love wine,", she cried.

Mummy stopped the Land Rover and we all climbed out. There was no sign of James or Daddy yet.

"We'll go in and have a drink," said the Colonel. "They won't be long now."

We sat in armchairs in an elegant lounge. Lisa couldn't stop giggling. Mary sized up the waiters. I talked to Ben about what we would do the next day. Half-term was ending. It seemed to have come and gone like an express train, and yet encased in it were some terrible moments none of us would ever forget. The Colonel refused help and brought us drinks himself on a tray.

He was a perfect host. He looked old and graceful, like some moustached pedigree dog. Eventually he sat down beside Mummy and talked. I had a cider to drink. I sat waiting, waiting for James. He came at last, pale and tall, one arm in a sling. He smelt like a hospital, but he was smiling. And now suddenly we were complete, a collection of people who had gone through something together. Only Mary didn't belong.

"They threw me out," said James, laughing.

"Not when they were going?" cried Mummy.

"Yes, and the road felt mighty hard when I hit it!"

The Colonel was fetching James a drink, talking to Dad at the same time, and suddenly he seemed younger and merrier, perhaps because he was feeling wanted at last.

"What did they say?" I asked.

"Not much, but they were hating me, and their language was something terrible, not what you would expect from the elegant Commander at all."

His face had sticking plaster and a dressing across one cheek. Mummy made him sit down.

"You weren't concussed, were you?" she asked.

He shook his head. "I can remember everything perfectly," he said. "The only problem is the moped. No one's found it yet and I promised to return it tonight intact."

Mrs Mills sat sipping whisky. Mike had chosen Coca-Cola. James went on talking, telling us how the man with the squashed nose had found him trying to slash one of the Mercedes' tyres, how he had bundled him into the car and tied him up, issuing the most terrible threats. Then the Commander had come, crying, "I've got the money! We'll beat it!" and leapt in, revving up the engine while the man with the squashed nose said, "I've got kids of my own – release the American boy first, do you hear? Or I'll grass." And the Commander had driven at tremendous speed towards the signal box, still not knowing that James was in the back.

They had left him there while they had gone to the signal box and found us. James had watched it all from the window, unable to get out because his hands and legs were bound with tape and the doors locked. He had tried shouting but no one had heard. He had tried to reach the horn, but that had been impossible, and then the Commander and the other man had come back. And two minutes later they had heard the police sirens.

"We travelled very fast," James said. "Over a hundred most of the time, I should say. It was very frightening. The Commander knew I was there by then. He wanted to shoot me. He called you all names, dreadful names – I can't repeat them," continued James, "and then without warning the Commander climbed over into the back and said, 'This will give me great pleasure,' and simply opened the door and threw me out."

"We must go in to dinner now," the Colonel said. So James stopped talking and we all trooped into a beautiful dining room with a high ceiling and lots of gilt.

And when we had finished ordering, which took a long time because no one could make up their minds, James continued: "It seemed ages before anyone came. A dog appeared first and jumped round and round and licked my face and barked; then a snail crossed the road; and then a woman with a little boy

111

came along. I heard the boy say, 'What's that, Mummy?' and Mummy said, 'A dummy.'

"So I yelled, I'm not a dummy. I'm tied up and I need help. My head was aching by this time and there was a pool of blood which I was lying in, so that my hair felt awful and my right arm felt completely numb."

"Don't tell us, it's horrible," interrupted Lisa.

"Mummy was very shocked," continued James, "and the little boy kept staring at me with eyes so wide that I was afraid they would fall out. Then Mummy started to run towards a phone-box, saying, 'I'll get help,' leaving me in the middle of the road for anyone to run over.

"I think she didn't fancy touching me, you know what some people are like – afraid of blood. I was feeling pretty funny by this time but I remember yelling, Untie me, please untie me. But she didn't stop, her horrible high heels went click-click on the road, and the little boy kept shouting, 'Wait!' "

James pushed away his plate of smoked salmon.

Lisa said, "Go on."

"There isn't much more to tell," continued James. "She never came back, not the Mummy and the little boy, but a man with a dog came on a bike and said, 'What's the matter, son? Are you all right?' The understatement of the year, I should say." The waiters were listening now, the whole dining room had fallen silent. No one seemed to be eating any more.

"So I said, No I'm not, mate. I'm b— awful. Can you untie me, please. He was an old man, and first he leaned his bike against a telegraph pole and then he called his dog, which was called Patch. And all the time the pool of blood was getting bigger. It was terribly frustrating. He was very old and his hands were knotted with rheumatism and I was done up with rope and some frightfully sticky tape, and he kept saying, 'I can't do it, son, I can't do it.'

"And then at last I heard a siren, and an ambulance came full of real people who had wonderful scissors and bandages and were calm and reliable. They said, 'Okay. We'll have you on a stretcher inside three minutes. Don't worry.' And they did. It was marvellous," said James, stopping at last. And the waiters started to work again and the other diners started to eat again.

Mummy leaned forward and kissed James. Lisa said, "It's like a serial on television, only worse. Did they wash your hair?"

"The nurses did. Everybody was fabulous in the hospital and they got onto the police. But of course it was all spoilt by me being sick. The nurses said it was delayed shock. It was very boring anyway. And then they wanted me to stay in for the night and we had a great argument about that.

"Anyway, here I am at last, with a cracked collar-bone, five stitches in my face and twelve in my knee, but otherwise not much the worse for wear. How are all the rest of you? What else happened?" finished James.

We told him as quickly as we could, but there was so much to tell, and it took a long time. Ben told about the Armstrongs and about what he told the police and how Mrs Armstrong couldn't stop crying. "I wanted to catch the Mercedes. I wanted to spit in the Commander's face, just once, but we took the wrong turning and missed the fun," he said.

I told about my ride home and about my passing out. Lisa told about the reporter who was so beautiful that she wanted to marry him, and Mike told about Cassandra's foal and how beautiful it was, the most beautiful thing he had ever seen. And suddenly we all felt happy, except for Mary, who bit her nails and shouted, "I want my camera back!"

Then the grown-ups had coffee and brandy and liqueurs, and James fell asleep in a chair. A middle-aged woman came up and said, "Excuse me. I couldn't help hearing what you were saying. Was it true?"

And I nodded and said, "You're not a reporter, are you?"

"No, dear, I'm not," she said, "But I think you all sound very brave. Is the dark-haired boy your brother?" I nodded and answered, "They both are," and pointed to Ben, and suddenly I felt proud of them, which was something I had never felt before.

The Colonel was paying for the dinner and Mummy was putting on her coat, and Dad was standing behind the Colonel now with his wallet in his hand, saying, "Let me help. Please." But the Colonel simply pushed him away saying, "This is my dinner party."

The moon was shining as we travelled home and we sang in the back of the Land Rover, sad, sentimental songs.

I thought, we can't go to school tomorrow because the Armstrongs are coming to say goodbye. The stable yard was full of shadows when we reached it. The Cummings' ponies were lying down and so was Cassandra, with her foal by her side.

Everything smelt marvellous, of horse and hay and summer. Bed felt marvellous too – like heaven. I undressed and pulled the bedclothes over my head and felt really safe for the first time that day. I thought, thank goodness it's over. All I want now is peace. And then I slept and slept and slept.

Eleven
The end of it all

When I wakened my room was full of sunlight. And I lay in bed thinking, everything's all right. Paul is with his parents, Cassandra is with her foal, James is alive, and I felt quite stupendously happy.

I dressed slowly, looking at the sunlight outside, thinking that at last summer had come in earnest. James was still in bed. Ben was mucking out. Mummy was in the kitchen stacking the dishwasher. "Bad news," she cried when she saw me. "Look!"

She held out a letter and all my sense of happiness started to wilt and die, and I thought, what now?

I took the letter, which was written on a piece of torn lined paper and read:

Dear Auntie, I have heard from my dad. He knows all about the kidnap. He knows something else and he wants me back. He is like the Commander and no good. I don't think you will want me any more when you know all. So I am going now. Thank you for everything. But I can't escape my past,
Mike

"What does he mean?" asked Mummy in a

distracted voice when I had finished reading. "As if things aren't bad enough without him adding to them."

"He's been so marvellous," I said. "He's mad to go back."

"I shall have to contact the welfare people," Mummy said. "I can't leave them in the dark."

"I'll go after him," I answered. "I'll bring him back. We can't manage without him now. You want him back, don't you?"

Mummy looked tired beyond words. "Yes. He must have got a letter this morning. He wasn't here when I came down," she said.

"When did the postman come?"

"Seven-thirty."

And it's nine now, I thought, and cursed myself for staying in bed so long.

I found my crash cap and ran to the stables. The yard was swept clean. Ben and Solitaire were missing. Lorraine stood waiting by the gate, her sides dirty with dried sweat from yesterday.

Mermaid whinnied hopefully. Cadet banged on his door, wanting to be noticed. I longed for time to "stand and stare" as I caught Lorraine and tacked her up, wondering where Mike would have gone, alone and worried at seven-thirty in the morning. He could have hitch-hiked miles away by now, or walked to Radcott and caught a bus somewhere, or met his dad in the village and gone for good. But he wouldn't have left a note then, I decided. He had left a note because he wanted to be followed.

We should have been at school. The village was quiet and empty. An old man was cutting the grass in the churchyard, his clothes the same faded colour as the older tombstones. Then I saw another elderly man sitting on the seat which had been presented to the parish at the time of the Coronation of Queen Elizabeth the Second, or so the plaque on it reads.

His name was Mr Parker, and I cantered across to him and yelled, "Good morning, Mr Parker. Have you seen Mike by any chance?"

He pointed to the woods, calling, "He wouldn't speak. I asked him why he wasn't in school, but he wouldn't speak."

I shouted, "Thank you," and gave Lorraine her head and tried to imagine how I would feel with his sort of father. And it will grow worse, I decided, as he grows more law-abiding. The woods were silent in the sunlight. Bluebells were out like a sudden blue carpet under the tall beech trees. I let Lorraine walk and thought about Paul. We were going to miss him, and if Mike never returned the house would suddenly seen empty. I remembered that none of us had wanted Mike and that we had suspected him of stealing. Ben had even accused him of it, but he had forgiven us. Then I saw him sitting on a stile, a forlorn figure staring across acres of green wheat, a rucksack on his back.

He heard Lorraine's hoofs and turned

118

round. "Why did you come?" he asked. "I don't need you. I can manage now."

"I thought you were going back to your father," I replied. "But you don't have to – we want you back. You don't have to be responsible for your father. It's not your fault he's like he is . . ."

He rubbed his forehead with a hand, leaving a dirty mark. "You don't understand, Harriet. 'E wants information. 'E wants help. He wants to know about your Mum's silver, and you know what that means . . ."

I started to laugh. "Mum hasn't any silver, she sold it all to buy sheets when we started the Inn. Come back, Mike. We need you," I said.

"You don't understand," he answered, getting off the stile. "I wrote to Dad when he was in prison, telling him about the place. I told him it was ever so posh, that kind of thing. And about Paul and all 'is pocket money and about the posh school he went to. I didn't mean no 'arm. I just wanted to let him know how happy I was . . ."

"It doesn't matter," I answered. "It doesn't make any difference."

"You don't understand," he said again, wiping a tear off his cheek. "The man with the squashed nose is one of his mates. I'm sure of that. They call him Fish Face, on account of his nose."

"You can't be sure, you didn't see him."

"It all fits, don't it?" he asked.

I didn't know what to say. For a moment

everything did fit, it was like suddenly finding the last bit of a jigsaw puzzle and putting it in place. We knew now why the Commander had come. And then I remembered the waiting, the suitcases which came first, the big build-up. I remembered Mummy telling us about the Commander and then about Mike.

"But the Commander wrote about coming long before you came," I cried. "He was delayed, that's why you came first. But the whole plan must have been hatched before you ever set eyes on the place. And the welfare lady sent you. Your father didn't have anything to do with it, Mike, so you're in the clear. You're okay!" I shouted.

"Are you sure?"

"Yes. Ask Mummy when you get back. The Commander's letter came before you did, long before you did."

"I've been a fool, haven't I?" he asked, walking homewards through the woods. "But it all seemed to fit."

I nodded. "It doesn't matter," I said.

"He used to beat me and he gave Mum a black eye, regular every Saturday," he said.

I didn't know what to say. He stopped and picked me a bunch of bluebells, though I would rather he had left them growing in the wood.

It was going to be a hot day, and above the trees the sky was an endless blue. "I think we need some fierce dogs," I said as we came to the common at last. "I must ask Dad." The bluebells were already wilting in my hand.

Then I started to run, leading Lorraine, remembering that the Armstrongs were coming to say goodbye. It must be eleven by now, I realized with growing panic. They've probably been and gone.

There was a big car parked at the front of the house, with a chauffeur pacing the drive. Lisa came running to meet us. "They're here!" she shrieked. "They brought Mummy a huge bottle of perfume and masses of flowers, and Dad the biggest bottle of whisky you've ever seen, and the Colonel a box of cigars, and Mrs Mills a book, and James a watch and me a fantastic book costing fifteen pounds about horses ... Honestly, they've gone mad, Harriet, they really have."

I left Lorraine in an empty box with her tack on and yelled to Mike to hurry.

James shouted, "Here she is," as I rushed into the hall, which was full of suitcases, and Paul said, "I wanted to tell you everything, but there isn't time now."

And I said, "I'm sorry. I wanted to hear what happened to you, but I had to go after Mike."

"We wanted to buy you something special, dear," said Mrs Armstrong. "Give it to her, Bill."

They looked very rich standing in the hall dressed for a journey. I looked at my old jeans and dirty boots and felt ashamed.

"I don't deserve anything," I said. "Please."

"We owe you a lot, Harriet," announced Mr Armstrong, stepping forward. "And we want you to accept this gift as a token of our esteem." And he took a necklace out of a case and put it round my neck.

He smelt of after-shave lotion, and Mrs Mills shouted, "It's opals, Harriet, real opals."

I said, "Thank you, thank you very much."

And Paul cried, "You saved my life, Harriet, no kidding."

"Ben was there too, and James," I answered. "But thank you very much. They're lovely."

Paul sat on a case, staring into my face and smiling. Mr Armstrong looked at his watch and shuddered. "We must get going, or we'll never make it," he said.

Lisa sat on the biggest case, yelling, "You're not going, Paul. I'm not letting you." Ben pulled her off.

Then the chauffeur came in and started picking up the cases. Mrs Crispin had arrived and was dusting the banisters and listening to everything. Mike stood clutching a ten pound note, Mary had some chocolates. It was like Christmas, but sad too, because now we were saying goodbye.

Mummy kissed Paul, Paul kissed Lisa, Lisa started to cry.

"You're all to come and stay – okay?" asked Paul in a shaky voice, beginning to cry too.

"We'll miss the plane," shouted Mr Armstrong from outside.

"Thanks, honey," said Mrs Armstrong, kissing me on the cheek, then kissing Ben and James and Lisa, saying, "I think you're the greatest family. I do really, the very greatest."

"We're not, we're hopeless," I answered, thinking that life must go on regardless of how miserable we were feeling now.

The chauffeur stacked the last of the cases in the biggest boot I had ever seen.

"You must come on a visit. We'll be living in the mountains right near the old Apache trails," called Paul.

"Be seeing you," I yelled.

They were waving now, going out of our lives, perhaps for ever.

"I am going to stay with them," Lisa announced. "I'm going to marry Paul."

"Not that again. I thought it was going to be the reporter," moaned Ben.

Everything was suddenly quiet now. Lisa wiped her eyes.

"Nice to have you back, Mike," said Mummy, turning towards the house.

"Nice to be back," replied Mike.

"They must have spent a fortune, an absolute fortune," mused Ben.

Dad was in the hall, looking at the newspaper. "Have you seen yourselves? Look, you're in it," he said.

I took it from him and saw myself sitting in the kitchen looking half dead, and suddenly I didn't want to remember that moment, it was too awful to remember.

"MYSTERY KIDNAP OF AMERICAN BOY," read Lisa. "And look at me." She stared at herself. There was another photograph of the house. "I look awful," she said. "My tummy is sticking out."

"It always does," replied Ben.

"What did Paul say?" I asked. "What really happened?"

"It's a long story, and we haven't much time," replied Ben. "Let's exercise the ponies and talk as we ride. The Cummings rang up to ask after their ponies and was I embarrassed!"

"I bet. What did you say?" I asked, searching for my cap.

"All sorts of tripe about them settling in very well . . ."

I felt happy suddenly, happy that it was all over, happy in a way I had never felt before. I wanted to sing, to turn somersaults, to shout, "Everything's all right. We're safe, alive, safe. And the Armstrongs are safe too." I wanted to thank someone for my happiness.

We were both running now, laughing, free of tension at last. We tacked up the ponies. I rode Mermaid because she was the smallest. She had a short, quick stride and didn't want to leave the stable yard. Her neck was thick, and dappled like a rocking-horse. Cadet went sideways all the time, which made conversation difficult.

"He needs to learn the turn on the forehand," Ben said. "He hasn't the faintest idea what my legs mean."

"What about Paul?" I asked.

"What about him?"

"What did he say?"

"That he ached all over."

"No, the story! What actually happened?" I shrieked.

"Well, the Commander was all right at first," said Ben, pulling Cadet into a walk. "He bought Paul lots of beer at the Crooked Billet and a pork pie and a bag of crisps, and Paul felt rather funny. Then they rode on and Paul felt funnier still, and then suddenly the Commander said, "This is where we leave the horses," and there was the Mercedes with Squashed Nose in it. And Paul says he said, "You can't just leave them here, they'll be killed, and what about the tack?" But our dear Commander just bundled him into the car and off they went, driving here and there for what seemed hours, and then ending up in a house which seemed to belong to Squashed Nose. It smelt terrible and the curtains were kept drawn all the time, and they ate nothing but sausages and mash, and Paul kept worrying about the horses but he couldn't do anything because one of them watched him all the time."

"Poor Paul!" I said.

"He was sure scared by this time," continued Ben, "but the Commander was very nice really. He talked politics all the time, mostly about a chap called Karl Marx, and they played cards, and then he had a drink of something which must have been drugged, because the next thing he knew he was in the signal box tied to a stool. He shouted and shouted, but no one heard. Then he started to pray and he was scared, and then he spent ages singing 'The Stars and Stripes' and thinking how great the United States is and how he might never see the land of his fathers again. And then suddenly he heard us and was he pleased!"

"No kidding ... So he didn't suffer too much?" I asked.

Ben nodded, shortening his reins. "He was terribly upset about the horses and Mr Armstrong wanted to pay for Cassandra's treatment – quite mad when we shouldn't have let Paul go out with the Commander in the first place. They could have sued us for negligence," replied Ben.

"Instead they gave us fabulous presents ..."

"That's Americans for you – they're so jolly nice," replied Ben.

"Touch wood, they may sue us yet," I cried, reaching for a tree trunk.

"They can't change their minds now," said Ben, laughing.

"I shall miss Paul," I said.

"Not as much as Lisa," replied Ben. "Did you read the paper?"

I shook my head. "It's peculiar, but I don't want to read it," I said. "I don't think they should make money out of other people's misery, do you? And it was misery, wasn't it?"

"It's all wrong in the paper anyway," Ben said. "They call Paul an ambassador's son."

We were trotting now and there was sunlight everywhere.

"The police say that the Commander is only an amateur at crime, and he certainly botched the kidnapping, didn't he?" asked Ben.

"Yes, but we mustn't call him the Commander any more."

"He'll always be the Commander to me," replied Ben.

"He's just a wolf in sheep's clothing," I said. "We must get some fierce dogs who know the difference . . ." And I saw us crossing the common with a couple of dogs running ahead of us, the house full of children and the exhaustion gone from Mummy's face, and suddenly life was full of hope again.